SECOND
CHANCE

by

Norman Sosner

NORMAN SOSNER

POETS ROAD
ISBN: 1936723018
ISBN-13: 978-1-936723-01-0
www.poetsroad.com

SECOND
CHANCE

*I dedicate this novel to my ever
supportive wife for her intuitive insights
and encouragement.*

NORMAN SOSNER

PROLOGUE

At 3 p.m. on a bright September day in 1944, the school bell rang and young Nicky Summers chortled gleefully as he ran to the exit gate to meet his Nanny Jo for their walk across the park to his home, where he knew his parents and grandparents awaited him with a birthday cake and candles in celebration of his sixth birthday. As they took their usual route, a small dark speck in the sky grew gradually larger, accompanied by an intermittent buzzing sound. Nanny Jo instinctively dragged Nicky into the brick shelter of the park's restrooms, partially protected by a wall of sandbags.

The buzzing sound grew louder then suddenly stopped for a brief, unnerving silence, followed by a tremendous explosion which violently shook the shelter and the ground around it. The pair, visibly shaken, emerged, and continued their walk, arriving shortly at the site of Nicky's home, now engulfed in a cloud of black smoke. Police and the volunteer air raid wardens looked grimly at the rubble of the store and apartment above it.

There were clearly no survivors.

CHAPTER ONE

Nicky's parents, Henry and Jean, had met at a suburban London dancehall in the summer of 1936, and began a year-long courtship which led to their marriage while both were in their early twenties. As a wedding gift, Henry's father installed the young couple in a three-story Victorian house in a North London suburb, with a store on the ground floor, a parlor and kitchen behind it, as well as three bedrooms and a bathroom on the two floors above. A small garden in the rear completed the residence. Henry and Jean worked hard to make a modest living, stocking the store with dry goods and sundries designed to meet the daily needs of the surrounding neighborhood.

Their baby son, Nicholas, was born exactly one year later, forcing the young working couple to seek help with both housekeeping and the care of their infant son. They could no longer rely on the generous assistance they had received from their parents, who were now busily engaged in running their own nearby stores. Jean and Henry contacted a domestic employment agency seeking a combination housekeeper/nanny. Soon thereafter, they were delighted to receive a detailed application and photo from a seemingly pleasant and well-qualified girl from a small Yorkshire mining town.

At the age of 18, Josephine Branscombe had been seeking an opportunity to advance her career, so she was intrigued by an advertisement placed in her hometown newspaper offering domestic employment in London. Leaving school at 14, she had worked part-time at the local Co-op store where her mother was a cashier, and she helped out at home with household chores and the care of her younger brother, Willy, recovering from polio.

Josephine was determined to make her own way in the world, and her hometown of barely 15,000 souls offered very limited opportunities in the depressed economy of the times. She did not care to work in the local woolen mill, and the only other jobs were in the coal pits where her father had slaved since his teen years.

Replying to the employment agency's advertisement she applied for the position of a domestic helper with the London family. She offered character references from her school principal and the manager of the Co-op store in Wombwell and was soon rewarded with a positive reply directly from the Summers couple. They were impressed with Jo's credentials, and were anxious to meet her personally. They offered her a return railway ticket with a probationary period of one month's employment as combination housekeeper and nanny for their infant son.

With nothing to lose, Jo excitedly accepted and prepared to take her very first trip away from her family and hometown. Parting with her family was a rather tearful affair.

"We shall all miss you, lass," said her mother. "Of course, we wish you the very best, and do hope you will write and let us know how you are getting on."

"Don't worry, Ma, I will be OK and I will definitely keep in touch. With a bit of luck I'll be able to come back for a weekend visit real soon."

The long journey—first by bus to Barnsley, then by train to London—took all of seven hours, and was by far the longest trip of Jo's life. Traveling modestly in third class, she was too excited to read, but whiled away the time by chatting with fellow passengers, and by enjoying the changing scenery of the English countryside from her corner seat window. She re-read her glowing testimonials and silently vowed to live up to them and make a good impression on her new employers.

For a short while she closed her eyes and dreamed of the London scenes she had seen only in magazines and occasionally in pictures at Wombwell's primitive little cinema, housed in a converted church hall. Her reverie was interrupted by the train's sharp whistle as it slowed and crawled the last mile or two into London's huge King's Cross station.

Clutching her small bag and purse tightly, she followed the other passengers to the end of the platform, where she was greatly relieved to be greeted by a tall, smiling gentleman in a navy blue trench coat who introduced himself as Henry Summers. "I recognized you instantly from your nice photograph," he said, "and of course the red beret you promised to wear. I hope you are not too tired from your long journey," he continued. "We still have a ways to go. Let me take your bag. We could stop for a cup of tea, if you wish."

"Oh no, really, I am too excited to be tired, and I am anxious to meet your wife and little boy," answered Jo.

"Well, then," said Mr. Summers. "Let's go down to the underground for the train to our North London suburb and then it's only a short tram ride to our home."

This news of a further complicated journey was a big surprise to Jo, but she prepared for what seemed like another huge travel adventure as they descended down the magical escalator into the bowels of the earth for a 30-minute ride on the "Tube," as Mr. Summers told her it was popularly called.

"You'll soon get used to it," he said. "Millions of Londoners ride it to work every day. You won't have to," he continued with a laugh. "It's much quieter in our neighborhood, and you can walk almost everywhere you need to." Jo was greatly relieved to hear this, and they soon boarded a double decker tram for the five-minute ride to the Summers' home.

"On a fine day, you can walk this little trip to the Tube station," confided Mr. Summers. Jo wondered silently how she would ever adjust to this huge city.

She felt quite at ease with Mr. Summers, and she was soon put equally at ease as she was greeted by his wife. "Hello, my dear," said Jean Summers. "Welcome to our humble little abode. It's so nice to see you safe and sound after your long journey. Let's all have a nice hot cup of tea and you can tell me all about it. I have some soup and a sandwich for you too, as I know you must be hungry. I bet you will want to see our little Nicky—he's asleep now,

but I'll take you in to take a peep at him when
I show you to your room."

"Yes, thank you Mam, I'd like that very
much," said Jo eagerly. She munched on her
sandwich, gratefully, drank her tea and stifled
a yawn. From her comfortable armchair,
Jo looked around the pleasant little living
room and decided it was anything but humble
compared to her family home in Wombwell.

Her first impression of her new employers
was that they were younger than she had
expected. Jean Summers was a pretty blonde
haired lady, only a few years older than Jo
herself, and her husband had already made a
good impression as he met and accompanied
her from the moment of her arrival. They,
in turn, were impressed with Jo's pleasant
disposition as they looked forward to a good
relationship with her.

"Let me take you up to your room. I hope
you will be comfortable there and get a good
night's sleep. Tomorrow you'll meet our little
Nicky. He's just starting to walk and I know
he'll keep you busy. We'll just look in on him
in his cot for a minute."

Jo was thrilled to see the baby who would be her charge, hopefully for years to come. "What a little angel," she said. "Yes, "replied Jean, but he can be a little terror when he's awake and running around. He'll certainly keep you on your toes."

"That's what I'm here for," said Jo. "I look forward to it."

"Well, good night, then, sleep tight" replied Jean.

"Good night, and thank you for your kindness" said Jo.

Downstairs, the Summers couple exchanged thoughts and agreed that Jo appeared to be just what they needed to take charge of their little son. "Let's hope Nicky takes to her, and she to him," said Jean. Tomorrow is the big day."

They needn't have worried, for Jo quickly endeared herself to both her infant charge and his parents, carrying out her duties with energy and enthusiasm. She even managed to soften her strong North country accent as she adapted to her new surroundings.

Though some might consider her rather

plain-looking, her luminous brown eyes gazed
directly at whomever she spoke with, and
her round open features framed by her short
brown hair, accompanied by a ready smile,
instilled a feeling of quiet confidence.

She played with Nicky and sang him to
sleep for his daytime naps, using the intervals
for numerous household chores, for which
Jean was truly thankful, giving her time to
assist her husband whenever he was busy in
the store. The so-called probationary period
was never referred to as Jo made herself
indispensable, and literally became one of
the family.

The outbreak of war in the autumn of
1939 offered new factory work back home
in Yorkshire and elsewhere, as well as
opportunities to join the Land Girls taking
the place of farm workers called to duty in
the armed forces. However, Jo had grown
so fond of Nicky, and he so dependent on
her, that she chose to remain in London with
the Summers family. She somehow always
managed to complete her household duties
and still have plenty of time to play with her

infant charge, bouncing him on her knee while teaching him to repeat his favorite nursery rhymes and singing him to sleep each evening. Accordingly, the Summers treated her as one of the family.

Although Jean Summers was an affectionate mother, Nicky always ran first to his Nanny Jo whenever he fell, bruised himself, or suffered a scrape. Jo did more than her share of work around the house. She cooked, baked bread and scones in front of the coal fire, and always had time for play. She had few friends, so apart from the occasional visit to the cinema, she preferred to spend whatever free time she had reading popular magazines and the novels of her favorite Yorkshire authors, the Brontë sisters.

Jo kept in touch with her family in Yorkshire mostly by correspondence, since the telephone was considered an extravagant expense reserved only for birthday and holiday greetings, or the conveyance of sad news. From her meager savings, she managed an annual visit by train on a long bank holiday weekend when the store was closed and she

could safely entrust Nicky into the care of
his parents.

Early in the new year of 1940 when Henry
Summers was called to join the army, Jo
became even more indispensable to the
family, and even volunteered to help Jean
in the store whenever Nicky was taking his
afternoon nap. Henry Summers soon shipped
off to France with the British forces. In the
summer of 1940, he suffered a leg wound
and was lucky to be rescued from Dunkirk in
a miraculous evacuation along with 350,000
British troops, vowing to return and
fight again.

To Jean's relief, his injury—though not life
threatening—kept him from further military
duty. With no more than a slight limp, he
soon resumed his work in the family store.
He also volunteered as an air raid warden to
help protect his neighborhood.

Though many young women with children
were evacuated to the countryside, Jean
remained with her husband and family as the

summer of 1940 was followed by a fierce German air assault on London. Nightly air raids were commonplace and refuge was sought in the basement of the house. Jo bedded down with young Nicky under the sturdy oak kitchen table, as she and Jean listened to the radio or read long into the night. Henry was frequently called outside to assist those neighbors whose homes were destroyed or damaged.

Both food and clothing were tightly rationed, making life in the store and in the home a considerable challenge. Somehow they carried on and were grateful that there was only minor damage to their home, primarily to the windows of the upper floors, as much from the anti-aircraft fire coming from the nearby park as from enemy bombs.

The aerial bombardment continued for the better part of three years, mostly by night, allowing life to go on in a nearly normal pattern, with the civilian population adjusting its daytime habits accordingly. Death and destruction were accepted in a stoic manner on the home front, while optimism regarding

the eventual outcome of the war increased
with the news of Allied victories, first in
North Africa, then in Italy, as well as on the
Russian front.

The arrival of American forces in England
in 1943 brought both encouragement and
amusement. Jean's older sister, Mary Maxwell,
a nurse in the local hospital, took on an
American boyfriend who was training for
his eventual dispatch to the continent. Nicky
and the family gratefully accepted the G.I.'s
generous supply of canned foods, tobacco,
and chewing gum, while the ladies reveled in a
supply of shiny nylon stockings.

At five years of age Nicky entered school,
having already learned to read, write, and
count through the tutoring of his parents and
by Jo, in particular. The occasional daylight
air raid, even by a lone bomber, was treated
with great diligence and respect for the safety
of the children as they were hustled into
the windowless gym, heavily protected by
sandbags. The entire population was supplied

with gas masks in brown cardboard boxes which they were warned to carry by string around their shoulders at all times when outside their homes. Although instructions on their use were given at the outset of the war, hardly anyone had ever bothered to examine them again, as the threat of an enemy gas attack appeared to diminish, although for no logical reason. Carrying one's gas mask case became a ritual akin to putting on one's shoes.

By 1944, a new aerial threat appeared—sporadic attacks by rockets in the form of pilotless planes. They made a buzzing sound on approach, followed by a sudden silence as they fell from the skies and eventually exploded indiscriminately on the ground. They were unaffectionately called "buzz bombs" or "doodlebugs" by the citizens, who were painfully aware that the sudden silence that followed that ominous buzzing sound allowed a scant few seconds to seek shelter.

When the buzz bomb destroyed Nicky's home and store, the rescue workers explained to Jo that there were no survivors. Though struck with horror, Jo's first thought was of the child's protection from the devastation they witnessed. Gathering him into her sturdy arms, she comforted him as best she could, momentarily putting aside her own fear. Sympathetic neighbors gathered around the scene of destruction, shaking their heads in dismay at the hopelessness of any rescue.

A kindly constable approached Jo, as he saw the tears streaming down her face and clutching the little boy close to her bosom. "Follow me, Miss," he said. "I'll take you to our police station around the corner, and you can rest up there for a while."

Jo just nodded in return, grateful for an arm to lean on and too bewildered to think beyond the moment. At the police station Jo was offered a cup of tea, and Nicky a jelly donut with a glass of milk. Recovering her composure, Jo asked permission to make a couple of telephone calls, the first to Nicky's aunt Mary, on duty at the hospital, and the second to her own parents in Yorkshire. Distraught and uncomfortable at the thought of breaking the terrible news to Nurse Maxwell, Jo still felt it incumbent upon herself to do so.

As Jo painfully recounted the afternoon's events, Aunt Mary was deeply shocked to learn of the loss of her only sister and parents. "Oh, my God," said Mary her hand to her mouth. "My poor dear sister and parents. No chance you say? I can't believe it. How awful. I'm simply devastated. And poor little Nicky, what a ghastly thing for him to witness, and on his birthday, too. How is he taking it?" she asked.

"Well, Mam, he's quiet now, but he had a good bit of a cry, and couldn't really understand what happened to his parents. I'm doing my best to comfort him, and the Women's Voluntary Service ladies are very kind, offering to give us shelter for the night. I'm so sorry for your loss, Mam, I felt I had to call you first. I'll do anything to protect my little lamb, and you'll be busy enough with the funeral arrangements. I'd like to save him from that, so with your permission, Mam, I'd like to take him up to my family in

Yorkshire till things settle down. I'll take him
to our doctor and maybe the parish priest
for counseling."

Mary was touched by the earnest and caring
young nanny. In her present predicament as
a wartime nurse, she regretted how little help
she could give to Nicky.

"Thank you, my dear, you are such an angel
and I know Nicky adores you. I wanted to
attend his birthday party this afternoon, but I
am on duty till late this evening. I know I can
trust you to do what is best. Give me your
number and I will call you in a few days and
see what I can do to help. Do you need
any money?"

Jo assured Mary she was all right for ready
cash and gave her number in Yorkshire. Mary
wished Jo Godspeed and thanked her again
for her concern before returning to her duties
in the hospital.

The volunteer women were kind and
generous with offers of clothing, even giving
Nicky a teddy bear, which he gratefully
clung to.

"Where are my mummy and daddy?" Nicky

asked plaintively.

Jo struggled for an answer. "They are safe in heaven now and the Good Lord will take care of them, darling," she replied as she held the little boy close to her chest and struggled to hold back tears. "Tomorrow we'll take a little train ride to visit my family and get some rest."

Jo called her family, who were shocked and horrified to hear the tragic news. They assured her of their willingness to do everything possible to shield Nicky from further tragedy. Early the next morning, Jo and Nicky went to the train station, purchasing tickets for the four-hour journey north to Barnsley. Upon arrival in the north, they were met by her mother's cousin, who escorted the pair to the local bus for the half-hour ride to Wombwell.

Nicky was very subdued, and shed no further tears. He seemed to be in a state of semi-shock. Jo decided to take him to the family doctor as soon as possible for observation and advice. She made up a cot for Nicky in her own bedroom, wanting to stay close to him and provide maximum comfort for the child, particularly should he awaken during the night. Exhausted and trembling, she climbed into bed and prayed fervently for strength and direction.

CHAPTER TWO

Jo's family home was modest and, like most of the semi-detached houses in the colliery town, offered rather cramped quarters. Her parents applauded Jo's courage and determination. Ma Branscombe assured her, "You were right to bring the little lad here, darling, we are so thankful that you are safe.

We are glad to have you back and we'll help to make a new home for Nicky."

Pa Branscombe had worked all his life in the pits, facing constant danger and surviving more than one mine disaster. He was staunchly supported by his wife, Emily, who augmented the family income by working as a cashier in the local cooperative store. Jo's younger sister, Daisy, was a bright and cheery girl who worked at the town's woolen

mill and, popular though she was with many
young men, seemed to have fixed her sights
on Alfred Bailey, currently employed as a
policeman. Brother Willy was recovering
from a childhood attack of polio, still too
weak to work and often buried in his books.
He willingly passed down some of his
childhood toys and clothes for Nicky, while
Daisy shared some of her clothes with Jo.
The local Women's Voluntary Service also
assisted with a variety of contributions.

Jo took Nicky to the doctor, who prescribed
a mild sedative for both of them to help them
sleep. To her surprise, Nicky refused to talk
about his parents and grandparents, never
even referring to the tragedy that cancelled
his birthday party and uprooted him from
everything that was familiar to him.

Though very shaken from the bombing
nightmare, Jo kept a steady head. She was
determined to help Nicky overcome his fear
and shock. To keep his mind occupied, she
enrolled him in the local school, St. Michael's
Priory, where he gradually adapted to the
broad Yorkshire accents and colloquialisms

of his schoolmates, and soon joined them in sports activities.

A few months after the bombing, Aunt Mary called Jo and, after asking about Nicky's adjustment, she said, "I cannot thank you enough, Jo, for all you are doing for my little nephew. With help from my hospital administrator I have contacted a reliable lawyer to set up a trust fund for Nicky's upbringing and education. He has agreed to act jointly with you as co-trustees to administer the funds resulting from the legacies left by Nicky's parents and grandparents. Do you think you could handle that?"

Jo was a little perplexed. "I don't have any experience in that area," she said. "What would I have to do?"

"I have a suggestion," said Mary. "How would you like to come down to London and spend a weekend with me at my place? We can talk things over, and meet with the lawyer so that he can explain. I will be happy to send you a train ticket. You are close to Nicky and know what is best for him. Being the co-trustee means that you will make decisions on his behalf as to how best to spend the money. You would simply consult with the lawyer and give him your best advice. I trust you to do the right thing for Nicky's future."

Jo was touched. "Thank you for your confidence, Mam, I will do my best."

"Thank you my dear. I don't know what we would have done without you and your kind family," said Mary. So you agree to visit with me soon?"

"Very well, Mam," said Jo, "I can get away next week if that is convenient."

"I look forward to it," replied Mary, and the date was set.

Mary met Jo at the railway station and took her back to her cozy little flat. Over a late night cup of tea, Mary spoke up. "Confidentially," she said," I am getting engaged to be married to my G.I friend. He is helping me to apply for immigration to the United States. It means a whole new life for me and I am so weary after working all those years in the hospital. I will keep in touch with you and hope that one day when we are settled, I can invite you and Nicky to visit us in Los Angeles."

"Well, congratulations, Mam. I hope you will be very happy," said Jo.

Mary continued, "There's a lot you don't know about me. I was married once before," she said. "I'd like to tell you about it, so that you would understand me better. After I left college, I went on a vacation to Italy and I met a handsome young man who literally swept me off my feet. I was crazy in love, and agreed to marry him, much to the dismay of my parents. His name was Aldo Macchione and I became Maria Macchione."

"For a while everything was fine, until he started staying out late and meeting with several young men with rather extreme political views. He joined Mussolini's Fascist Party and then the Italian army. Suddenly I was left alone and the final blow came when he told me he was being sent to Spain to help Franco's forces. I didn't know much about the civil war in Spain, but my old college chums were very liberal and terribly opposed to Franco's revolution.

"I was so scared, I ran away and came back to England. My parents wouldn't talk to me, but my sister Jean was very understanding and asked me to stay with her for a while. I was so happy for her when little Nicky was born."

Jo listened in sympathetic silence to Mary's harrowing tale while Mary continued, "One day I received a letter from Aldo's parents telling me that he had been killed in the fighting in Spain. Naturally I was devastated. I changed my name to Maxwell and took up my nursing career. Then came the war and I met this kind and gentle G.I. who offered me the chance to start a completely new life in America. I do feel a little guilty about leaving, but perhaps now you understand my situation better."

Jo was visibly moved by Mary's story.

"I do understand Mam," she said, "and I wish you all the happiness you deserve. You can rest assured that I will do everything in my power to look after Nicky. He seems to be adjusting well to our family life in Yorkshire. I will look forward to meeting the lawyer tomorrow, and learning my duties with the trust."

"Thank you so much for listening, Jo, I have complete confidence in you." The meeting with the lawyer went smoothly, papers were signed and Jo returned to Yorkshire a wiser and more mature young woman.

As the autumn months gave way to the Christmas holidays, Nicky made a few friends with boys his own age. Jo decided to invite a few of them to the house for a Christmas party. Pa Branscombe cleaned away his accumulated coal grime and donned a Santa Claus outfit, distributing sweets and small gifts to the youngsters and his family. Nicky presented a charcoal drawing of a house with a smoking chimney, which to everyone's great relief resembled the house in Yorkshire rather than his former London home. After months of therapy and loving care, he was adjusting to his new life and seemed to have buried his worst memories deep within his soul.

That winter, Daisy's friend Alfred taught Nicky to play football, and during the summer holidays taught him how to play cricket.

He took him on his motorbike to hunt
rabbits on the moors and for fishing trips
in the nearby River Dare. Both trips helped
augment the family dinner table, and provided
some excitement and fun for the little boy.

Jo's brother Willy also pitched in, sharing
his books with Nicky and helping him
improve his reading skills. Then, in the
summer of 1945, the six-year war ended
amid boisterous celebrations with balloons,
bunting, and street picnics.

Jo wrote to Mary, happy to report on
Nicky's progress. She learned by return that
the Mary was now ready to emigrate to
the United States with her new fiancé, the
American G.I. Out of courtesy, Jo asked
Mary permission to have her family formally
adopt Nicky, and received a grateful approval
in reply.

Transitioning from a perky little cockney boy
from North London to a young Yorkshire
tyke was not easy for Nicky. Traumatized

by the brutal loss of his family, he remained withdrawn and slow to trust strangers. One thing that helped his gradual adjustment was his attachment to the caring Jo. She comforted him from the jokes and barbs he received from his school chums, most notably because of his accent.

Fortunately Nicky overcame these obstacles because of his prowess in sports. The protective arm of Daisy's boyfriend, Alfred the policeman, was a sufficient warning to potential bullies. It helped Nick gain acceptance and overcome the irrational, ingrained Yorkshire fear of "outsiders." Alfred taught him to develop his natural gifts for football and cricket, and he soon became an indispensable member of the school teams.

Gradually making friends with his teammates, he quickly adopted their fondness for Yorkshire "butties and chips," even smattering his conversation with the occasional "owts" and "nowts."

In September 1945, he celebrated his seventh birthday with a party, together with a few of his new friends. In an uncharacteristic display of emotion, Nicky spoke up.

"Thank you all for giving me this lovely birthday party. I didn't have one last year because of the bad things that happened to my mummy and daddy, and my grandparents. I do miss them all, but you are my family now and I love you very much."

It was the first time he had mentioned the tragedy, and it appeared to be an indication that he was learning to cope with the bad memories. Jo had difficulty stifling back a tear and ran over to hug him, much to his embarrassment in front of his friends.

The next four years passed swiftly as Nicky grew taller and stronger. In common with his friends and all Yorkshiremen, he worshipped the legendary cricketer Len Hutton, the England captain who had set a scoring record for his country in the 1938 Test match against Australia. He was also a big fan of the new Yorkshire legend Freddie Truman, noted for his fast bowling achievements, who was a role model for Nicky, whose own strong right arm showed great potential.

He excelled in cricket, while he was also achieving good marks in his general school studies in preparation for his entry into Wombwell High School at age 11. In one cricket match between two sides chosen at random by the sports master, Nicky, as bowler for his team, faced a burly young tyke with a reputation as the school bully. Everyone feared Ernie Trubshaw as he strode to the wicket and faced Nicky at the bowler's end.

Scowling at the players around him, Ernie looked towards the boundary in preparation for a big hit as Nicky began his run at the other end of the pitch. Nicky took a few steps and hurled a furiously fast ball at his opponent. Ernie's confident grin turned to shock as his middle stump flew out of the ground and the wicket-keeper yelled a triumphant "Howzat?" The umpire raised his hand in agreement, "Out" he cried, as the astonished and humiliated Ernie was summarily dismissed.

Later, during the interval, Nicky was sipping a lemonade as the still scowling Ernie

approached him menacingly. The other boys
went silent, expecting Ernie's raised arm to
strike at Nicky. Instead, he put his arm around
Nicky and said "Good job, me lad. Next time
I want you on my side." The spell was broken,
and from that moment Nicky and Ernie were
friends. With Ernie as his new protector,
Nicky gained the respect and admiration of his
schoolmates. His confidence grew accordingly,
and was reflected in both his studies and
sports activities.

With less need to look after Nicky, Jo
went to work in the local day nursery, a
job for which she was so well suited. She
passed on her talent for sketching to Nicky,
who amused his classmates with simple but
artful caricatures. Under the guidance of Mr.
Osbourne, his sports master, he learned to
throw the javelin farther than any other boy,
with the strong right arm he had developed
from his cricket mentor, Alfred. He learned to
appreciate art and music under the guidance
of Miss Winters, the art teacher. It surprised
no one when Nicky was awarded a scholarship
to the local grammar school, and soon began

early studies for entry to university.

As a result of continued hard work and natural abilities, at the tender age of eighteen, Nicky earned a major scholarship leading to entrance into Peterhouse College in Cambridge. Although he also faced conscription for National Service because of his age, his teachers impressed the military authorities to grant him deferment until he could complete his degree course. From eighteen to twenty-one, Nicky applied himself diligently to his studies, specializing in International Finance and Law. With his strong desire to travel outside his own country, he felt that these courses would provide him with a secure profession as well as an opportunity to visit far-off lands.

CHAPTER THREE

Peterhouse was the oldest and smallest college in the Cambridge University system, founded by the Bishop of Ely in the year 1284. No doubt due to its relatively small size—with less than 400 attendees including graduate students—it had also gained a reputation for being the friendliest college in Cambridge, a major factor in easing Nicky's transition from his more humble background. It provided the ideal environment for Nicky to grow both in his studies and in sports. In particular, he distinguished himself with the javelin, winning the college championship at his second attempt, and also earning himself a place on the cricket team.

Recruited into the college boat crew for the strength of his arms, he was a regular and reliable oarsman. His closest friend was Colin Jarman, also a member of the boat crew. Both young men proudly participated in the annual May Bumps, in which the crew bumping the most boats went to the head of the river and were feted accordingly by their fellow students.

Dining in the 700-year-old refectory imparted a vivid sense of history and was amazingly inexpensive compared to other colleges, a factor which was particularly important to Nicky, coming as he was from rather humble circumstances.

Nick's meager allowance, combined with his observance of the traditional Yorkshireman's thrift, did not allow him to extend much hospitality. But in return for the friendship extended to him by his colleagues, he managed to host the occasional wine and cheese party.

Though beer was the beverage of choice back home and also in the college dining room, Nick took a keen interest in French wines, notably those of the less expensive variety, with help from the kindly proprietor of a local wine store. As a result, his comments and knowledge impressed a small coterie of fellow wine lovers, and together they appreciated Nick's occasional soirees.

Over time, Nick softened his acquired Yorkshire accent and began to feel more comfortable with his colleagues who had attended the trendier public schools.
In fact, as a mere grammar schoolboy of modest means, he gradually adopted a more sophisticated style of dress, speech and habits - without the snobbery of those who had been artificially protected from the common man.

There were very few female students at Cambridge at the time, Newnham and Girton being the only all-female accredited colleges at the university, and no ladies were admitted to the historically male colleges.

Newnham and Girton's visiting rules were so strict, young men were inclined to seek female companionship from the nearby Homerton Teachers' Training College, where they found willing partners for the occasional dance or social. Nick arrived on one particular occasion to pick up a partner for a dance. While being kept waiting for several minutes in the Great Hall, he was enchanted by the softly seductive sounds of Debussy's *Claire de Lune*, played by a student practicing piano for the school concert. The haunting melody remained in his mind for years to come, and at least on this occasion, provided a fitting beginning to a pleasant evening.

His attractive date for the evening was Anna Mackie. So agreeable did he find Anna, that he invited her to the May Ball—an elegant affair at which white tie was the de rigueur form of dress at Peterhouse. The ball celebrated the conclusion of the May Bumps and this year, the recent victory of Nick's crew.

So enamored was Nick with Anna, that he soon invited her to accompany him by punt up the River Cam to Grantchester for the traditional Tea in the Apple Orchard. There he recited the famous Rupert Brooke poem, pointing to the church tower clock still stopped at ten minutes to three, as the poet remembered. "I'm very impressed," said

Anna, "and I thank you most heartily for a most memorable weekend."

In the weeks that followed, Nick and Anna completed their studies. Awaiting the results of their final exams, they managed a few more casual dates. One day, while lazing on the banks of the River Cam, Anna confided to Nick, "You know, I am really going to miss you. I have to tell you that I have accepted a teaching post in the Scottish Highlands."

"Wow," replied Nick, "that does sound a bit remote. I am going down to London for a couple of interviews and I fully expect to settle there. What is the Scottish attraction for you?"

"Well, you know I come from a long line of Scots, and I have several relatives living in Edinburgh and even north of there in Aberdeen. But the job is way up in the Highlands at a unique private school for emotionally disturbed children. It has been of special interest to me in my training and although it is a bit of a challenge, I think I can make a useful contribution to their education."

Anna paused as a boat passed them by. "I was recruited when the principal came to Homerton searching for a willing prospect. He is a fine man, a Scot, of course, and I think we bonded on the spot."

There was little Nick could say, except to wish her good luck in her new career. He would miss her lively company too. "I am not leaving till next week," Anna continued, "and I hope we will stay in touch. I have promised to visit my elderly Granny this coming weekend. Would you like to cycle over there with me for tea? She has a nice little cottage about five miles upstream."

"Why certainly," replied Nick. "I've put my bike up for sale, but it hasn't gone yet. I don't fancy weaving my way on a bike through London's busy streets."

"That's settled then," said Anna. "I'll ride over to you about 2 o'clock on Friday, since her place is more out your way than mine."

Granny's little cottage proved to be quite charming in its old fashioned way, and the

dear little lady was obviously pleased to have
visitors. She had set a table by the window
with an embroidered cloth, her best china
teacups, and flowered plates from an
earlier era.

Apart from the usual little finger
sandwiches, she baked her own scones, which
she liberally spread with thick clotted cream
and homemade strawberry jam. "Oh, Gran,
you shouldn't have gone to so much trouble,"
exclaimed Anna. "This is truly delightful,"
said Nick, appreciatively. "Just like my own
home in Yorkshire."

"You are both very welcome," replied the
old lady. "It's really no trouble at all." She
brought out an album of family photos,
which Anna perused carefully. Nick strolled
out into the tiny garden, admiring the neatly
trimmed flower beds which Granny explained
were lovingly tendered by her neighbor. "I
can't bend down anymore," she said, "and my
eyes are not too good, either. Thank heavens
for John, next door."

After a couple of hours passed, Anna
detected that her Gran was visibly tiring.

"Well dear, I guess we must soon be going." Just then the skies darkened and a loud clap of thunder shook the little cottage. It was followed by a streak of lightning and big splashes of rain lashed against the windows.

"Oh, my," said the little lady, "you can't possibly go out in this. You'll be drenched on your bikes, and likely catch your death of cold. Nick, you help me light a fire in the grate, and you must stay until it's over. There's plenty of books to read, and I've got my sewing." She would not hear another word, and so Anna and Nick prepared to stay the rest of the afternoon.

It was an unusually fierce summer storm, and looked like it might well last into the evening, so Anna and Nick had little choice but to accept the old lady's invitation. Around 7 o'clock, the storm appeared to have abated, and the young couple prepared to leave, but more thunder and lightning returned and the rains became even more intense. "Well," said Granny, "it looks like it's in for the night, and

I won't hear of you leaving. You must stay
overnight and keep me company."

Whereupon she put on a frilly apron and
said, "There must have been a reason I made
a big bowl of beef and vegetable soup, and
baked a loaf of fresh bread too. Now you
have to stay and be my guests for a home-
cooked supper." Anna and Nick had no
choice but to humor the dear lady, and they
all sat down to enjoy the unexpected meal.

Anna cleaned up and Nick had to force
Granny to retire to her armchair and rest,
while he helped with the dishes. "Now you
know, Anna," she said, "I sleep down here,
and there's my nephew's room upstairs for
you, and Nick can bed down in my old sewing
room. It's a bit small, but the day bed in there
is quite comfortable. I can't see to sew any
more tonight and I am getting tired, but I
have something for you two to enjoy."

So saying, she brought out from the
cupboard a bottle of Tawny Port. "I've been
saving this since last Christmas," she said,
"and this as good an occasion as any."

"Well," said Nick, "That's very nice of you,

but we won't drink alone. You must join us in a glass yourself."

"Oh, if you insist," she smiled mischievously, "But just a wee drop to help me sleep."

They drank a toast and she toddled off to her sleeping alcove behind the kitchen. Nick stoked the fire as the storm continued to rage.

"What a lovely old lady," he said wistfully to Anna. "You know, I can barely remember my own grandparents. They died in an air raid when I was just a kid." With the bottle of port between them, they snuggled down on the rug in front of the fire, and reminisced about their respective childhood years.

Upstairs, they retired to their rooms, anticipating an easy sleep after finishing the port. "Nighty night, sleep tight," said Anna. "You too, my dear," replied Nick, "And thanks for a lovely day, even if it is a beast of a night out there. What is it they say? 'Any storm in a port'? Oops, I mean, 'Any port in a storm.' I think I've had a bit too much to drink." Anna giggled a barely coherent reply and gently closed her door.

A short while later, there was a tapping sound at Nick's door, and a visibly scared Anna entered, climbed onto his bed and said, "I've always been afraid of the thunder and lightning ever since I was a little girl. Do you mind if I join you?"

"I thought you'd never ask," replied Nick, hugging her close to his chest on the narrow bed. They did not even notice that the storm had passed.

A watery sun awoke them early next morning, and they hurriedly dressed, Anna taking care to tidy up and remake the beds. Nick went downstairs, cleared out the grate and took the ashes out to a bin in the garden. Granny came in and thanked him profusely, while she made herself her morning cup of tea. "I hope you slept well," she said, "I suppose you'd both prefer a nice cup of coffee."

"Thank you," replied Nick, "I'll just make us some toast and we'll be on our way. Anna is making up the rooms and will be down in a minute."

As the young couple bade their farewells,

Granny kissed them and said "It was lovely to see you and I do hope you will visit me again soon." Anna promised to return at least once more before leaving for Scotland.

Nick smiled thoughtfully and wondered silently whether he would see either of them again. Anna was headed for her teaching job in Scotland, and Nick prepared for the upcoming interviews in London, which would inevitably lead him to his new career.

They arranged a farewell dinner date on the following weekend, vowing to keep in touch, but it was a fact of life, that even after years of close contact, few college friendships survived the inevitable dispersion to distant places in the pursuit of different careers…

Fortunately for Nick, conscription for National Service was terminated just in time for his graduation, so he set about following his tutor's recommendations and sat for several job interviews. His family in Yorkshire was thrilled at the successful conclusion of Nick's educational training.

At a big party with his grammar school friends and teachers, the Branscombes bade him farewell and wished him every future success. It was Nick's opportunity to speak eloquently of his love and gratitude for all that he owed to the Branscombe family. He had rapidly matured into a sophisticated man of the world, which belied his humble roots.

His friend, Colin, decided to visit cousins in America, little anticipating that it would lead to his marrying an American teacher in Chicago and his appointment as an Assistant Professor of Law at nearby Urbana University. Other colleagues from his college days went their separate ways, few of them ever to meet again, as they each pursued new careers. Nick sat diligently through several interviews with prospective employers and was eventually recruited by the J. William Townsend Company, a prestigious finance and banking house specializing in international investments.

At his first interview with Bill Townsend, Nick was asked "What exactly interests you about joining our company?"

"Well," said Nick, "I studied hard to obtain my degree in Finance and Economics, but it was all very academic. I feel that I need some practical training in the real business world. I've done some research into your company and it's clear that you are a respected leader in your field. If you are willing to give me a chance, I'm prepared to work hard and learn from your experience. And I hope I can then make a significant contribution to your firm."

"Good," replied Townsend, "When can you start?"

"Just as soon as possible," said Nick. "I am ready to go and I have no commitments. I just need to find a convenient bed-sitter and a suit of clothes befitting a financial executive."

Townsend smiled and said, "Fine, I think we can help locate a place for you to stay. We haven't yet discussed salary."

"I leave that to you, sir," said Nick. "When I've proved my worth, we can talk again."

"Fair enough," said his new boss. "That's the spirit!"

Nick accordingly rented a modestly priced furnished apartment in central

London and made a few shopping trips
to acquire a suitable new wardrobe for a
young professional.

Nick and Anna exchanged Christmas cards,
and she enclosed a picture of herself and
the principal of her new school, a tall fellow
with a striking mop of red hair and a beard to
match. Nick thought she looked a bit plumper
than when he had last seen her in June.

Other college friends were scattered to
different places, and Nick suddenly found
himself alone in the big city. He applied
himself to a course of intensive training with
his new employers, working long hours and
with little social activity. He had considered
the option of post-graduate studies at his
college, but concluded that the real life
experience with the Townsend Company
better served his needs, as well as contributing
a regular source of income. For the first
time in his life, he was truly on his own, and
though his new bank account grew slowly, it
provided a comfort zone he had never
before experienced.

Socially, he missed the cocoon of his

small college and the circle of friends he had enjoyed through sports activities. He worked long hours gaining knowledge of the intricacies of international finance and the development of venture capital opportunities, which was the specialty of his new company. Returning late in the day to his little flat, he was usually too tired to do more than prepare a simple meal and read himself to sleep. He managed to keep fit with early morning walks whenever the weather cooperated, and he visited a local pub from time to time with one or more of his co-workers. He studiously avoided close contact with the very attractive secretarial staff, knowing full well the problems that could create.

On weekends he would join a couple of co-workers for a make-up game of football or cricket, and sometimes to see a professional match as well. Although he was socially at ease, he did not make close friends easily. The next Christmas, he received another card and photo from Anna, this time cuddling a small, red-haired baby girl, with Mister Red Beard standing proudly by her side. "Well," thought

Nick, "she said they had 'bonded' when he recruited her from Homerton. I guess life in the Highlands was lonely." He wrote a note of congratulations, and that proved to be their last contact.

CHAPTER FOUR

The decade of the '60s began with the first man in space and ended with the first man to walk on the moon, a triumph of American scientific genius and determination. It was a decade in which youth cast aside the complacency and conservatism of the immediate post-war era of the '50s. The period was often known as "the Swinging Sixties," associated as it was with the birth of British pop music and revolutionary styles in fashion. From Elvis to the Beatles and on to the Rolling Stones, a new culture of youthful exuberance dominated the social scene. Detroit produced the Motown sound, and fashion spawned bouffant hairstyles and mini-skirts, to the delight of the young and the dismay of their elders, who were even

more shocked by the new sexual freedom.
It was also a decade of huge advances
in technological inventions, notably the
computer age. Television spread to almost
every household in Britain and America, and
with it, a greater awareness of global affairs.

The coming of age for post-war baby
boomers was the beginning of a social
revolution which spread change and
influenced dress, music, and general behavior.
In sport, the English footballers defeated
the Germans to win the World Cup, and the
Englishwoman Virginia Wade astonished the
Americans by defeating the legendary Billie
Jean King in the U.S. Tennis Open, later going
on to victories in the Australian Open and
culminating in her triumph a decade later at
Wimbledon, witnessed by Queen Elizabeth
celebrating her Jubilee year.

Olympic champion Cassius Clay
changed his name to Muhammad Ali,
and demonstrated his opposition to the
Vietnam War by refusing to serve in the
military, later winning acclaim as World
Heavyweight Boxing Champion. America

was going through a catharsis with violent
demonstrations against the Vietnam War and
a decade of unrest leading to a landmark Civil
Rights Act—but only after the horrendous
assassinations of the two Kennedys and
Martin Luther King, Jr. Britain was shocked
by the brutal torture and murder of two
children on the Yorkshire Moors at the hands
of Ian Brady and Myra Hindley, both of
whom escaped the death penalty only because
it was abolished by Parliament just before
the scheduled execution date. As a mark of
human progress, the first heart transplant was
successfully carried out, and the emerging
computer industry was about to change the
way in which business and human contact
would operate.

In these turbulent times, Nick Summers
made progress in his career, enjoying constant
air travel in pursuit of business deals, with
little time to enjoy much social life or the
vibrant musical shows imported from
Broadway to the West End stage. He was by
no means anti-social, but his occasional flings
with members of the opposite sex were not

serious and merely served to pass the time.
He attended a few of the annual alumni
reunions at Cambridge, but became bored
with too much drinking and reminiscing of
"the old days." He soon gave up answering
the invitations. He had a number of friendly
acquaintances, including some among his
fellow co-workers, but he had very few real
friends who, like himself, were 100 percent
involved in their careers and often out
of town.

The technological advances provided
fertile territory for venture capitalists,
anxious to be in at the beginning of exciting
and potentially rewarding opportunities.
This was the relatively new field in which
Townsend specialized and which particularly
fascinated Nick. Following a couple of years
of intensive training, Nick began to travel to
the continent with assignments to explore
the new electronic developments in Holland,
Germany, and France. The British economy
was still in a slow recovery, but the new
computer age was the latest "Big Thing."
In fact, the acknowledged father of

computers was a Cambridge alumnus named
Alan Turing, celebrated for his part as a
decoder during the war years, which helped
the British turn the tide against the Germans.
By the mid-'60s, Nick was an expert in
researching innovative companies ripe for
investment, but too new or experimental
for the major banks to support. Townsend
provided a nest of wealthy individuals ready
to take a gamble in the hope of huge rewards,
and Nick's job was to bring them together.
Since nine out of ten new ventures were
destined to fail, Nick's ability to sort the
wheat from the chaff was highly regarded
by his employers.

CHAPTER FIVE

In 1968, Townsend sent their rising star
Nick Summers to Los Angeles to attend
a worldwide conference, at which a major
topic was the growth of start-up companies,
particularly in California where Stanford
science graduates were creating astonishing
new inventions often in their basements or
garages, notwithstanding the acknowledged
advances of large companies such as Hewlett
Packard and IBM.

Taking advantage of a few days leave, Nick
decided to pay a long overdue visit to his
Aunt Mary, now married to the American
G.I. He presented them with a basket of
fruit and vegetables and a bouquet of flowers
he had picked up at the farmers' market,
expressing his thanks for their care packages

sent periodically to him and the family in
Yorkshire. He told them about his upbringing,
his education, and finally his prowess leading
to his current job in the field of finance.
They were without children of their own, his
aunt spreading her motherly charms among
the children at the hospital, and her husband
coaching Little League, of which there was
ample photographic evidence in the living
room of their modest ranch-style home in the
San Fernando Valley.

"First, let me thank you for all you did
for me in setting up the trust fund for me.
Without that I could never have achieved
the proper education, nor the fine job I
now have."

"That was the least I could do for you,"
said Aunt Mary. "I confess I felt a little guilty
about running off to America and leaving
you, although I knew Jo would take good care
of you."

"Not at all," said Nick, "you were right to
pursue your own life, and Nanny Jo proved
to be a wonderful surrogate mother. I am
happy to see you and Stanley so well settled in

America. I can see that you have a good life here." Mary and Stanley exchanged smiles.

"You are always welcome here," said Stanley. "Stay as long as you like."

"Thank you, I would really like to spend more time with you both," explained Nick, "but as you can understand, I am on limited company time, and I have projects to pursue in both the wine country north of here, and especially in the Santa Clara Valley area, where some amazing inventions are taking place which may well change the way in which the whole world does business in future."

With a few tears and much regret, Aunt Mary said they understood, and they wished him Godspeed, with the hope that he would return.

He drove on up along the coastal road to Santa Barbara, where he was fascinated by the influence of the Spanish architecture which gave the city its unique look. His immediate objective was to explore the Santa Ynez Valley north of the city, where a burgeoning wine industry was creating a number of small wineries needing investment to help them compete with the older, more established ones. The reliably sunny days and cool ocean breezes created an ideal climate for the vineyards, some of which were already competing favorably with the French, and with fewer problems of crop disease. Together with wineries in the Napa Valley, they were utilizing innovative scientific techniques that were attracting the attention of their competitors in Europe. So far, however, they lacked the financial and marketing skills which would make them universally accepted beyond California. Nick visited growers in Santa Ynez and Los Olivos, and prepared a report for Townsend's investors, enjoying numerous stops at the friendly tasting rooms.

Continuing northwards, Nick took note of the many small start-up companies introducing new developments and software techniques in the growing computer industry. The area was ripe for investment and he reported accordingly to Townsend. His time was limited, and he hoped he could return for a more detailed investigation. For now,

he had to move on to San Francisco for his
return flight to London.

CHAPTER SIX

Back in London, he was soon caught up in a whirlwind of meetings and business activities, again leaving him little time to think about his social life. It was not until the summer of 1969 that a unique opportunity presented itself. Keenly aware of the remarkable technological achievements emanating around the Stanford campus and the surrounding Santa Clara Valley, Townsend decided to send Nick back to the region to investigate in more detail the investment landscape. More and more the small start-ups were challenging the supremacy of the established companies like Olivetti, Bell Labs, and Hewlett Packard. Some of them had the potential to produce enormous profits for those willing to take on the risk of early investments. Nick's job was to conduct painstaking research and report his findings accordingly. It was a daunting task, which he accepted with relish.

With a weekend at leisure, Nick took advantage of an opportunity to break his journey in Chicago in order to visit his old chum Colin Jarman, one of the very few of his college friends with whom he had remained in touch. Colin was now married to an American teacher and celebrating the birth of their second child. He welcomed Nick warmly and, over a uniquely American backyard barbecue, they reminisced and brought each other up to date.

"You certainly seem to have settled down quickly in America," commented Nick.

"Indeed I have, old boy, it's a great life," replied Colin, "and I was lucky to have found the right girl to share it with. We have wonderful friends and neighbors and two adorable kids. Family and friends, that's what it's all about. When are you going to settle down, Nick?"

"You were lucky," said Nick, "I just haven't found the right girl, yet."

"Well," said his friend, "you work so bloody hard running all over the place."

"I enjoy my work," replied Nick, "but when I do find the right partner, I'm ready for a quieter life."

"Well, good hunting," said Colin. "After all you've gone through, you deserve a happier and more settled life."

Nick marveled at the way Colin had adapted to family life and new community friends, reflecting wistfully that he had yet to put down any roots himself. His life was one round of business travel after another.

Bidding farewell to his old friend, Nick realized that he may have left insufficient time to catch his flight to Los Angeles. He had barely an hour to get to the airport, but he was hopeful that the taxi he ordered would manage to navigate the heavy traffic. The sweltering midsummer heat in June was causing many problems, with asphalt roads crumbling and cars overheating. His driver, a heavily accented foreigner from some Eastern European country, used every curse in his

limited vocabulary as he wove in and out of
the congested lanes, eventually managing to
deposit Nick at the terminal less than twenty
minutes before his scheduled flight departure.

Nick approached the check-in desk, then
flashed his ticket on the counter, depositing
his suitcase on the weigh-in scale. "I'm sorry,
Sir," the check-in agent said, "I'm afraid you
are too late, and your seat has been given to a
stand-by passenger. I'm afraid that's the airline
policy within 15 minutes of departure time."

Nick was non-plussed and barely had time
to complain before the agent smiled and said,
"Hold on a moment, the coach section is full,
but I can just manage to upgrade you to the
last available seat in First Class if you hurry
to the departure gate and take your bags
with you."

Nick muttered a brief "Gee, thanks" and,
lugging his suitcase with him and tucking his
large briefcase under his arm, he ran all the
way to the gate and just managed to board
in time. An obliging flight attendant took his
suitcase and parked it in one of the forward
compartment lockers. Breathlessly moving

down the aisle, he spotted his allotted seat in the last row of the first class section, noting that the window seat was already occupied by a flight attendant. The doors closed as Nick flopped into his aisle seat and fastened his belt for take-off.

His seat companion turned to him and said, "Well, that was a close call." She was a very attractive young lady, sipping her complimentary glass of champagne. Nick was quickly provided a similar glass and held it aloft in a toast. "Well, here's to a pleasant flight," he said, as the plane taxied down the runway. Secretly, he could not believe his good fortune: first, the free upgrade, and now the loveliest—and apparently friendliest—seat companion he could wish for. They were soon handed elaborately decorated menus with a wide choice of entrees. Nick was busily studying his, as his companion turned and offered a suggestion.

"I can recommend the filet of beef," she said. "They carve it from a whole tenderloin."

"I gather you are familiar with this flight," Nick replied, noting she was wearing the airline's uniform.

"Yes, I am dead-heading to my home base in San Francisco, but first I'm stopping off for a day to visit my grandfather who is in a hospital in Los Angeles."

"Oh, I'm sorry. I hope it isn't serious," said Nick.

"Well, I am afraid it is," she replied. "He has just undergone surgery, but we're hoping for the best."

"Please allow me to introduce myself," said Nick. "I am Nick Summers, and I have just been attending a conference in Chicago. I stopped off to visit an old college friend. Now I am on my way to California to explore business opportunities for my company."

"And what kind of business is that?" asked his companion.

"It's a relatively new field called 'venture capitalism' replied Nick.

"Hmm, sounds quite intriguing," she answered. "I wish you luck."

"From your accent I gather that you are English, so welcome to our country. My name is Louise Linden and, as you can see, I fly for United and I'm transferring from cross-country duty to the Pacific route from San Francisco to Hawaii."

"That sounds magical," said Nick, entranced. "You know, Hawaii was actually discovered by an Englishman, though he called it the Sandwich Isle—a Yorkshire-man too."

"Is that especially significant?" asked Louise, a bit puzzled.

"Oh, just a bit of hometown pride," laughed Nick. "I was brought up in Yorkshire, and we love to boast about our heroes, although in truth I was actually born in London."

Over the excellent roast beef dinner, Nick and Louise continued their easy conversation. "I was a war orphan and I lost my family in a bombing attack. I was only six at the time and my Nanny took me to her family in a small coal-mining town. They adopted me and so I was raised and nurtured there. Hence my Yorkshire pride," said Nick. "Please, tell me something about yourself," he ventured.

"Well truthfully, there isn't a whole lot to tell," said Louise. "I never knew my father—

he was killed near the end of the war in
Europe a few months before I was born.
I have very few relatives, actually. I just grew
up in San Francisco and applied for a job with
the airline, hoping to see a bit more of the
world. As a novice, however, I was assigned
to domestic routes and so the Hawaii transfer
is about as exciting for me as I can get. I have
done a couple of training flights there and am
really looking forward to it. Spending a night
or two there is better than Cleveland
or Detroit."

Nick could not take his eyes off his friendly
companion. Her long, wavy blonde hair, her
neat figure and facial features, especially her
bluest of blue eyes, and not the least her
smiling disposition—all of it captivated his
attention, as they continued to while away the
flight hours in a charming and chatty manner.
Shortly after they crossed the Rockies, the
pilot made an announcement that startled
the passengers.

"I have to report that we are experiencing
a minor problem," the pilot said. "We are
having a little trouble with our fuel pump

and as a result, we are leaking fuel. There is no need for alarm, but as a safety measure I am afraid we shall have to make a landing somewhat short of our destination Los Angeles, most probably it will be in Las Vegas, which we shall be approaching quite soon. I will advise you all in a few minutes, after we make contact with the authorities there."

Nick and Louise exchanged glances. "Well, that's a place I've been longing to see," said Nick.

"Me too," replied Louise. "I wonder how long we'll be there." Her question was soon answered by the pilot's announcement. "We ask you to remain seated when we land, until we can verify how long we shall be on the ground at the Las Vegas airport. Please be patient while we make that estimate."

A few minutes later, the passengers were advised that repairs would take several hours, so the flight could not resume its journey to Los Angeles until early next morning. Overnight hotel accommodations would be provided to those who requested them, as take-off next morning would probably be around 6 a.m. Nick had a sudden idea.

"How would you like to join me in a whirlwind tour of the casinos and hotels?" he ventured to ask. "I'll be happy to rent a car, and together we can explore as much as possible. I understand everything is open 24 hours in Las Vegas, perhaps we can see a midnight show, have an early buffet breakfast . . . and forget about sleep for one short night. It is already after 10 p.m. and we shall have to report back at the airport for the flight to Los Angeles by 5 a. m."

Louise was startled by his suggestion, but it appealed to her sense of adventure. "I'm game, if you are," she said to his delight. "I only have an overnight bag, we could put it with your luggage in a coin locker when we land."

"Good thinking," said Nick, and he proceeded to rent a small car for their midnight jaunt around Las Vegas.

Following a suggestion by the car rental agent, Nick drove straight to the Strip where they were in time for the late show at the

Sands Hotel. Sinatra and the Rat Pack put on a brilliant performance full of hilarious comedy and outrageous antics which left Nick and Louise in high spirits.

"Gosh, I'm hungry," said Nick, "Let's find one of those bounteous buffets I've heard so much about."

The nearby Flamingo Hotel, true to its reputation as one of the first major resorts in Las Vegas, did not disappoint, and after their meal they tried their hands at numerous slot machines in the dazzlingly huge casino in the hopes of hitting a jackpot. A few small wins kept them happy, but unsuccessful in the search for a big win.

"Let's try our luck somewhere else," suggested Louise. "I've still got a pocket full of coins."

They laughingly continued their adventurous hunt for riches at the newly opened Caesar's Palace. An hour or two later, they had gone through their coin collection, but agreed that it had been very good fun. Exhausted, they flopped down in the comfortable lounge for a pre-dawn respite before reluctantly making their way back to the terminal for the early morning check-in. Neither of them believed they could have enjoyed so much fun in each other's company after their chance encounter just a few hours earlier. On arrival in Los Angeles, each were forced to go their separate ways—Louise to visit her grandfather in hospital, and Nick to his aunt for a quick visit before continuing his business assignment. With a parting hug, they exchanged cards, expressing the hope they would soon meet again, though they both silently wondered how and when, considering the oceans that separated them.

CHAPTER SEVEN

Driving up to the Santa Clara Valley, Nick made contact with several new start-up companies, eagerly listening to their plans for remarkable technological breakthroughs and trying to determine which of these young entrepreneurs would best merit the involvement of the investors represented by the Townsend Company. He continued his drive north to San Francisco, before embarking on another major project which would take him to the Napa Valley vineyards and then on to New Zealand.

The Hawkes Bay and Marlborough area wineries in that country showed great potential, but lacked the financial resources to bring their wine products to the attention of the world markets. From his

early experiments in wine tasting, Nick had
expanded his knowledge of the industry,
so much so that this project was close to
his heart. He had made a personal study of
climate and soil conditions in France and
the potential of the New World wines
intrigued him.

Combining his knowledge of wines with his
training in the investment field encouraged
him to pursue the assignment entrusted to
him by Townsend, even to the extent that he
might make some personal investments in the
process. The reluctance of banks to make the
necessary loans to these wineries presented a
window of opportunity for venture capitalists
seeking new fields. He checked in to the St.
Francis Hotel and immediately called United
Airlines in search of Louise. Her business
card had been burning a hole in his pocket
ever since he left her in Los Angeles.

Fortunately, she was not only in town, but
taking a few days leave and she welcomed him
with great enthusiasm. "How nice to see you
again so soon," she enthused. "Allow me to
show you around my wonderful city." They

spent a joyful day of sightseeing, riding the cable car to Fisherman's Wharf to sample the fresh seafood, winding up with peals of laughter at one of the popular comedy clubs in the North Beach area, and concluding with a late-night supper at an Italian bistro.

Nick explained that he was bound for the Napa Valley prior to his trip to New Zealand and invited Louise to join him for a pleasant weekend among the wineries.

"Nothing like combining business with pleasure," he laughed, "and on an expense account too." Louise needed little persuading.

For the next couple of days, they drove through the area, visiting those small wineries previously selected by Nick for his special assignments, but they also had time for some fine dining and wine-tasting. In Yountville they enjoyed a champagne brunch in the gardens of the lovely Domaine Chandon vineyard and sampled the culinary delights of a restaurant with the intriguing name of "The French Laundry."

Heady with champagne, they now faced the awkward moment when it was time to decide where to spend overnight. "I have an aunt and uncle who live in Vallejo," said Louise. "They have often spoken of an historic resort called Silverado. We could try there," she offered. Nick noticed a certain hesitancy in her voice, and he said "OK, we'll see if they can accommodate us. I have a feeling you would prefer two single rooms."

Louise smiled coyly "Well, I wish this was not our very first date, you know what they say about nice girls on first dates."

"Yes, I have heard," laughed Nick. "So let's not spoil your reputation."

"You are the perfect English gentleman," said Louise, with gratitude. They managed to obtain two tiny single rooms at the iconic hotel, ruefully noting that they were in what appeared to be former service quarters. "Let's enjoy a nightcap in the lounge, it will help us both sleep," said Nick. "Agreed," replied Louise. "It has been a marvelous day, and I have enjoyed your company enormously. Let's meet for breakfast on the terrace tomorrow, say around nine?"

"It's a date," replied Nick. "I have a few

choice wineries to show you before we head back." He kissed her gently on the cheek and, bidding her "Good night," resisted the temptation to linger.

Next morning was the usual warm and sunny day in Napa, and they drove North to visit the Chateau Montelena Winery, where Nick pronounced its Cabernet the rival of any French wine he had ever tasted. Following lunch at the Calistoga Inn, they observed a boisterous group in a large communal outdoor spa, then rode the cable car to the hilltop Sterling Winery, from whose summit they enjoyed a superb view over the entire Napa Valley. On the way home, they stopped for wine-tasting at the newly opened Robert Mondavi winery, outside St. Helena, enchanted to find they were in time for a twilight concert by a charming young pianist. Once again Nick heard the haunting strains of *Claire de Lune*, and he told Louise where he had first heard it in Cambridge.

"It seems to follow me wherever I go," said Nick. "Yes," replied Louise, "it is quite a lovely and haunting melody."

Louise was enchanted, and not just by the romantic music. Nick was totally different from the often lecherous types she frequently encountered during her airline duties on domestic business flights. She truly wanted to pursue this relationship.

On the late evening drive back to San Francisco, she suddenly had an inspiration. "Look," she said, "tomorrow I am due to fly to Hawaii to attend the wedding of my friend Malia. I know you are bound for New Zealand, but I am familiar with the transpacific flight schedules, and I believe it is possible to arrange a brief stopover in Hawaii. I would love you to accompany me to the wedding as my escort. Do you think you could do that?"

Nick was taken aback by the sudden and intriguing invitation. He, too, wanted this relationship to continue. "I would be delighted to stop over with you in Hawaii even for a day or two. I will cable my firm in London and see if they approve a minor change in my timetable."

TransPacifica Airlines flew directly from

Honolulu to Auckland three times a week and together they checked availability. Townsend wired back an "OK" to proceed, and Louise explained that her friend Malia operated the beauty salon at the hotel in Honolulu where the airline crews frequently stayed. She and the hairdresser had quickly become friends, and Louise was sure Malia would readily agree to Nick's accompanying her to the Hawaiian wedding.

Back in his room at the St. Francis Hotel, Nick found it difficult to sleep. His weekend trip to Napa was paying unexpectedly rich dividends.

Twelve hours later they embarked on the five-hour flight to Honolulu, where they met Malia in the terminal, greeting additional guests. She welcomed them both with hastily procured leis and, assuming they were a couple—which they did not deny—promptly called her fiancé Kimo, an entertainer at the iconic Coco Palms hotel in Kauai, to change Louise's room from a single to a double. Together they embarked on the half-hour flight to Kauai, where the wedding was to

take place the next evening. Nick gazed in
wonder at the tropical setting of the famous
hotel with its palm-shaded lagoons, recalling
that it had been the setting for the Elvis
Presley movie, *Blue Hawaii*.

A lazy day on the island preceded the
wedding festivities. Nick and Louise took
a boat ride up the Wailua river to the Fern
Grotto, where the romantic *Hawaiian Wedding
Song* was sung for the admiring tourists.
"What a place for an idyllic wedding,"
said Nick, to no one in particular. Louise
smiled silently in agreement. Everything was
conspiring to bring them closer together.

On the wedding eve, the girls had a last-
minute bachelorette dinner, and the groom
and his friends invited Nick to join them in a
beer binge with lots of Hawaiian appetizers,
called "pu-pu," at which Nick tried hard not
to laugh, and the celebrations went on far into
the night. By the time Nick staggered to his
room, he found Louise fast asleep.

The wedding day was the usual bright and
sunny one. With no wedding ceremony until
the early evening, Nick and Louise toured the

island to the awesome Waimea Canyon and to the sleepy little village of Hanalei, where they learned that the movie *South Pacific* was filmed. They swam off the sandy beach where the fictional Nellie Forbush "washed that man right out of her hair." Louise, however, had no such plan for Nick.

Returning to Coco Palms, they attended the lavish luau and wedding ceremony of Malia and Kimo. Flushed with multiple Mai Tais and a liberal champagne toast, they wandered off to the beach for a moonlight swim. Exiting the surprisingly chilly waters, they raced up the beach and flopped down. Nick wrapped a towel around Louise's shivering shoulders as they hugged each other closely for additional warmth. Their passions aroused by the romantic scene, and finding the beach deserted, their embrace developed into gentle lovemaking, which continued long after they returned to their cozy room.

An early morning sun glinted through the window shades and woke Nick from a heavy slumber, surprised to find himself alone in the room. Stumbling into the bathroom, he noted that Louise's toiletries had vanished and there was no sign of her clothes and suitcase. He spotted a note on the dresser which simply said:

"Hated to leave you Lover Boy, but had to dash to the airport to resume my schedule. Thanks for a lovely weekend.

Till we meet again, your Louise."

Nick smiled wistfully as he recalled their "wedding experience" with very fond memories. No one had ever made such an impression on him, and he mused about pursuing a future life with this wonderful girl.

With several hours free before his flight to New Zealand, Nick refreshed himself with a swim in the hotel pool, enjoyed a snack lunch, and purchased a flower bouquet and a bottle of Veuve Cliquot, which he left with a note of gratitude to Malia and Kimo for their gracious hospitality and what he described as, "the best experience of my entire life."

On his free afternoon, Nick attempted to write a letter to Louise, but found it difficult to express the intensity of his feelings. He speculated on the possibility of a future life with her, recognizing the fact that they lived so far apart. Would she contemplate relocating to England? Undoubtedly he could help her find work, utilizing her excellent people skills. How could they plan to see each other more frequently? Would a marriage proposal appeal to her or were they rushing things?

In their brief time together he felt that their mutual love of music, art, and travel, along with the ease with which they communicated, suggested a very promising relationship. He had no doubt that he had fallen in love, and he resolved to test that love as soon as possible.

In the meantime, he had to complete his assignment to investigate the investment possibilities in the fledgling wine industry of New Zealand. Perhaps he could manage a stopover in San Francisco on his way home? For the first time he had difficulty expressing himself coherently, as he had more questions than answers. With his mind a whirl of conflicting thoughts, Nick prepared to board his long flight across the Pacific to Auckland.

CHAPTER EIGHT

He settled into a comfortable aisle seat over
the wing of the aircraft, folded his jacket and
placed it together with his briefcase into the
overhead compartment, hoping for a quiet
and restful flight. As more people boarded,
he found himself surrounded by a boisterous,
laughing group of high-spirited young men,
evidently a team of athletes returning from
a mainland event. Their noise was soon
enhanced by the delivery of cocktails served
shortly after take-off.

Nick strolled to the rear of the aircraft and
found a row of empty seats which offered a
more restful experience. He relocated, then
made his choice from the menu handed to
him by a smiling stewardess. He also chose

a glass of Fume Blanc from New Zealand,
which reminded him of the same wine he had
discovered with Louise at the Mondavi winery
in Napa.

She continued to dominate his thoughts as
he bedded down for the night with a blanket
and pillow. He did not know how long he
slept, but he was awakened by the violent
buffeting of the aircraft by exceptionally
strong turbulence, accompanied by huge
flashes of lightning. A voice from the cockpit
urged passengers to tighten their seat belts
as more of the same was expected until they
could rise above the storm.

Suddenly, a bolt of lightning struck the
port-side engine, which alarmingly burst into
flames. The pilot tried to calm the passengers
as he struggled to keep the aircraft on an even
keel, but Nick could not recall such a violent
storm in his many years of travel. It was clear
that the aircraft was lurching from side to side
and losing altitude.

Further discouraging news from the cockpit
urged all passengers to check the location
of life-vests under their seats, as there was a

possibility that the aircraft, so far from land,
might have to ditch in the ocean. More flashes
of lightning occurred as the plane bounced
from side to side. A loud crack in the middle
of the cabin revealed a gap in the roof
of the fuselage, and luggage from the
overhead compartments flew among the
terrified passengers.

Many reached for their life-vests and Nick
quickly put his on, preparing for the worst.
The gap in the ceiling grew wider and with a
rush of air, the mid-section of the cabin blew
apart, scattering bodies in all directions. The
tail section where Nick was seated broke off
as the crippled plane plunged towards the
ocean, and Nick blacked out.

Hours—possibly even days—passed before
Nick awoke in a blaze of sunshine, finding
himself parched and sunburned, floating in
calm seas in the middle of the Pacific ocean.
He was totally disoriented and had no idea
how much time had passed. He continued to
drift in and out of consciousness, aware only
that he was terribly alone.

He hardly felt the strong hands of local

fishermen hauling him into their boat, muttering in strange voices as they steered him to safety on their remote little island. When he finally regained consciousness, he found himself in a tent being fed coconut juice by the gentle hand of a Polynesian native girl, who was also bathing his face and head with tender care. She handed him a flask of cool water, which he drank with trembling hands.

"Where am I?" he asked, but she did not appear to understand and simply smiled in return.

A burly Polynesian man approached him, and in a heavily accented French voice he said, "Bien venue a Manihi. Qui etes vous, Monsieur?"

"Manihi," murmured Nick. "Je suis . . ." he started. Then he stopped, as he could not complete the sentence.

Who indeed was he? He had no idea. His memory was completely gone, yet he welcomed the chance to speak in French. "Manihi, ou est il?" he asked. He sat up and eagerly took in a few morsels of food and more water to quench his thirst.

He soon learned that Manihi was a tiny coral atoll in Tahiti, about 300 miles from the capital of Papeete. It was populated by a mere 72 souls and ruled over by the Chief—the burly man who had addressed him in French. The Chief was puzzled by Nick's inability to explain his identity, except to say that he was an Englishman who fortunately spoke French.

When shown the tattered remains of his life-vest, Nick made out the name of the airline and realized that he had been involved in a disastrous crash, yet he still could not recall the events which led up to it. He also did not know what he was doing on the plane in the first place. He was acutely aware that he was a victim of amnesia, undoubtedly brought on by his terrifying experience, though he also realized that he would have difficulty explaining it to these simple but friendly islanders.

For the moment, he was intensely grateful for their kind hospitality. Hopefully, in their care, he would grow stronger and regain his memory. Certainly it seemed apparent that they were not overly concerned about his past and they treated him as an amusing curiosity, with tolerance bordering on affection. In the absence of a name, they called him "Monsieur Anglais." His wounds were carefully bathed, and he was freely offered the fruits and vegetables grown on the atoll, as well as the abundant varieties of fresh fish.

Nick gradually regained his strength as he swam, even diving for the precious black pearls which were the main source of the island's economy. He joined in simple sports to the delight of his native hosts. He amazed them with his dexterity in throwing spears from over 150 feet to bring down coconuts from the profusion of palm trees. A vague thought crossed his mind that he had done something similar to this in his earlier life, but the details escaped him.

Back in San Francisco, the news of the airline disaster made headlines with few details, other than the aircraft had run into a violent storm and crashed somewhere in the Pacific with no reported survivors.

SECOND CHANCE

Louise was totally devastated, and she fell into a deep depression. She forced herself to return to work, but could barely go through the motions of attending to her passengers. With support from her fellow attendants, she managed to get through those first couple of weeks only with great difficulty. Off duty, she shunned company and frequently sobbed herself to sleep. She sought help from her regular doctor, though his prescriptions were of little use.

As weeks went by, she was unable to shake off the blues, and her flight companions noticed dark rings forming under her eyes from lack of sleep. She began feeling nauseous during flight, as she never had before. On her next visit to the doctor, she faced the realization that she was pregnant. Her first thoughts were to terminate her pregnancy, but as time went on she not only accepted the fact, but began to welcome the idea that she would give birth to Nick's baby. Unable to face her companions, and unable to hide her condition, she felt obligated to resign from the airline without further delay.

Her mother had recently succumbed to cancer, so Louise felt that her whole world was collapsing. She was determined to get away somewhere where she would not have to face friends and make explanations.

She contacted her Aunt Grace and Uncle George in Vallejo, a smaller city north of San Francisco. They were an elderly, kindly couple who agreed to take her into their home and help her prepare for the birth of her child. Having lost a son in the Vietnam War, they welcomed their niece with great generosity. Uncle George was an Agricultural Inspector for the nearby Napa Valley vineyards and, through his contacts, he introduced Louise to the director of a wine consortium seeking an assistant. Louise was happy to find work and start a new life, at least for the next several months.

Her baby was due sometime in April, and she felt she was able to work at least through the winter and early spring. She hoped to be able to continue her new work after a short leave to have the baby. Aunt Grace promised to be a willing and loving nanny.

Louise adapted rapidly to a quieter life in the relatively small town atmosphere of Vallejo. She soon made friends with her co-workers, who were all anxious to promote the fine quality of their local wines. The short commute was an easy drive, and the absence of pressure enabled Louise to regain her natural glow and good health. Apart from the occasional disturbing dream and her longing for Nick's presence, Louise slowly tried to accept the tragic event which changed her life.

CHAPTER NINE

Stranded in Tahiti, Nick was gradually gathering strength. One day, he noticed a group of natives gathered around a small battery operated radio, astonished by the news of a man landing on the moon. They shook their heads in disbelief, pointing to the sky and muttering, "La lune, la lune." They considered Nick a little crazy as he tried to explain the scientific experiments which led to this achievement by the Americans. He then made a mental note of the date—July 20, 1969—as he reflected on the number of days he had been on the island.

The monthly freighter arrived from Papeete, bringing supplies of fuel and food, as well as a bundle of outdated newspapers. Nick

anxiously scanned them for news of the
airline disaster, but could find no account
of it. One of the men did mention that
he remembered hearing a radio report of
an airliner crashing into the ocean with no
survivors some weeks earlier. Nick continued
to suffer repeated nightmares about an airline
crash, but he could not remember his part in
it. It seemed that no one on the island had
bothered to report his miraculous escape and
rescue by the local fishermen.

He enjoyed deep sea diving and fishing for
the black pearls, though on one occasion,
Nick hit his head on a submerged rock,
causing him to suffer a concussion, fever,
and severe headaches. After a day or two, the
Chief became concerned and ordered his
men to take Nick by longboat to the capital
of Papeete, where he could receive
hospital treatment.

He was admitted as "M. Anglais" and
tended to by the kindly Doctor Emile
Moreau, a French physician who recognized
Nick's amnesia and worked patiently with him
over several weeks of therapy.

As Nick quickly recovered from his concussion, he learned that his form of amnesia was unlikely to be permanent. It was described as "source amnesia" brought on by extreme trauma, meaning that Nick would not lose all of his background and business knowledge, just the source by which he acquired it. It was only a matter of time that something would eventually trigger his memory of the more recent chapter of his life that was temporarily blocked.

The kind doctor lived in a fairly large plantation house, and upon being released from the hospital, Nick was offered the use of a tiny cottage on the grounds. Dr. Moreau became more than just Nick's personal physician. He became a good friend with whom Nick dined frequently and played cards.

Moreau introduced him to Bruce Collins, a British expatriate who acted as the volunteer Honorary British Consul in Tahiti. By coincidence, he was a Cambridge graduate who had settled in Tahiti as a result of his father's activities as a professional yachtsman.

Bruce confessed to Nick that, though his
stay in Tahiti had been intended as merely
temporary, he had become so enamored
with the tropical life—its natural beauty and
French-flavored culture—that he settled
into a local law practice and indulged in all
the culinary and artistic delights to be found
there. Additionally, and most significantly,
he had married a charming young Tahitian
lady who taught art at the local school. With
a small colony of other British expats, he
enjoyed representing them as the unofficial
British Consul.

Nick began taking classes from Bruce's
wife Tia and soon became proficient in
painting watercolors of local scenery, which
he occasionally sold to visiting tourists. From
this supplementary income he was able to
return some of the hospitality he had received
from his mentors, Dr. Moreau and Bruce, by
treating them to a lunch or dinner.

Through Bruce's contacts, Nick was offered
temporary employment in an export/import
business, which gave him a small, but regular,
income. This enabled him to purchase a few

clothes and personal items.

To legalize his activities, Bruce used his contacts with the local French government officials, asking them to be patient regarding Nick's status as a recovering amnesia victim without a resident's visa.

News reports of that fateful airline disaster, some few hundred miles away, had indicated no survivors, though it seemed obvious that Nick was indeed a lone survivor of that crash. Bruce obtained a manifest of the passenger list, but unfortunately, none of the names triggered any recognition as to which of them might be Nick, still dubbed Monsieur Anglais, but now with the added nickname of "Jacques." Establishing his true identity was a major priority for his rehabilitation.

Speaking to Nick about his own days at Peterhouse in Cambridge, Bruce showed Nick an old copy of one of his alumni magazines. Thumbing through the slightly discolored and faded pages, he came across some photographs of the college boat crew and athletic champions. Peering closely, they both stared at the figure of a lean, crew cut young

man who bore a likeness to Nick, whose
current long hair and beard masked
his features.

"Shave off that beard and cut your hair,"
joked Bruce, "and that could easily be your
double." Nick stared thoughtfully at the
young student poised in the act of throwing
a javelin. He also looked at the faces of the
boat crew celebrating their victory in the May
Bumps. He told Bruce about his prowess in
throwing spears at coconut trees with the
young men in Manihi, and resolved to shave
off his mustache and beard that very evening.
Returning to the astonished Bruce next day,
they both perused the magazine photos
and captions.

"By Jove," exclaimed Bruce excitedly, "It's
you, old boy. You must be Nick Summers, our
javelin champion of 1960."

"I did not know you personally," Bruce
went on. "I may have been a year or so
behind you, but I certainly cheered on
your sports efforts." Now 30 years of age,
Nick had gained weight, but his features
were unmistakably like those of the young

student in the photograph. "This calls for a celebration, old chap. We must call Dr. Moreau immediately."

Then he asked, "Do you recall your student days now?" Nick's reaction was one of startled puzzlement mingled with the hope that this was the beginning of his recovery from oblivion.

"I'm trying, Bruce, I'm really trying," he said, "but everything is so vague in my mind. The javelin certainly seems to ring a bell, and I had that fleeting memory of it when I was spearing coconuts on Manihi. You have been enormously helpful and I can't thank you enough."

Bruce could not hide his own excitement and promised to make further enquiries. "If that is indeed you," he said, "Peterhouse will have a complete record of your admission records, your date of birth, family background, etc. and then we can establish your identity without doubt."

That night Nick dreamed of punting on the River Cam, studying in college, and taking part in various sports. When he awoke, he

realized his dreams were not fiction, but the
reality of his former life. It still puzzled him
that his other memories were so vague. Over
the next few weeks, under Dr. Moreau's care,
he worked hard to recapture the details of his
life. Bruce continued to feed him information
of their days together in Cambridge,
prompting Nick to reach back to remember
his life before and after college.

Checking the airline manifest again,
Bruce found the name Nicholas Summers
as a passenger, thus validating the identity
he had helped establish from the college
photographs. Together, they waited patiently
for the information anticipated from the
college admissions office. Dr. Moreau
continued to encourage Nick and told him
that before long, something would happen
to trigger his memory. He assured him that
it would return naturally, as in most amnesia
cases. "Just be patient, mon ami."

The report from Peterhouse was a goldmine
of information, the most vital of which
was the address of his adoptive family in
Yorkshire. Nick wrote immediately to Jo to

inform her of his miraculous rescue from the plane crash, taking care to tell her about the nature of his amnesia and the expert treatment he was receiving in Tahiti.

Her joyous reply, along with a family photo taken with him at a previous Christmas celebration, stirred recognition and memories of his upbringing. Dr. Moreau was delighted at this progress, as Nick struggled to recall his life after graduation. Jo's letter gave him the information and address of his employers, the Townsend Company, so he wrote to his boss, Big Bill Townsend, with the news of his rescue and present status in Tahiti.

Within a couple more weeks, he had corresponded again with Jo, learning news of the family. Daisy had married Alfred and produced a baby son whom they named Nicholas. Albert, suffering from emphysema, had retired from the colliery and Jo, true to form, was spending her spinster years caring for him. Ma Branscombe still worked at the Co-op store and Willy continued to read voraciously. They all prayed fervently for Nick to return speedily to full health and visit them.

Bill Townsend wrote that he and the firm
were devastated when they first heard about
the plane crash and were now planning a
huge celebration party for Nick's return. Nick
was thrilled to hear that his job was safe and
promised to keep them informed as soon as
he could manage to leave Tahiti for England.
There was still a problem with his lack of a
passport, which could only be issued by a full
British Consulate. Bruce's advice was for Nick
to travel to New Zealand, where the nearest
British Embassy could obtain verification
from the U.K. authorities, and issue the
document. Nick wrote to Townsend with this
information and received in return the details
of his original assignment to investigate and
report on the New Zealand wineries.

All of this activity was re-energizing Nick
and helping him recall many details of
his recent past. He now knew he was on
his way to New Zealand on behalf of his
company, when the plane crashed, though
what he was still missing were the events
which immediately preceded his flight. Dr.

Moreau assured him these memories would soon follow and pronounced him otherwise physically fit.

Describing his amnesia problem to Townsend, Nick begged them to provide him with as many details as possible regarding his activities on their behalf immediately before the flight. Consequently he learned that he had visited computer companies in California and then checked into the St. Francis Hotel in San Francisco. He was told that he had requested permission to change his flight plans in order to attend a wedding in Hawaii, and permission had been granted accordingly.

Attending a luau that evening in Papeete, Nick experienced a strong vision of another luau. That night he dreamed about the wedding luau in Hawaii and, most notably, the presence of a beautiful girl who accompanied him. There was laughter and drinking and there was a beach scene, and together they were swimming in the ocean—but he could not remember her name, and her face kept drifting in and out of his vision. The vividness of his dream remained with him the next

morning, and he felt instinctively that he was
close to recovering his memory, especially of
the girl who seemed to be the central character
he most wanted to remember. If only he
could recall her name, he was sure he could
locate her. If they had travelled together to the
wedding, surely the airline would have a record.

That evening while dining with Dr. Moreau,
he was offered a glass of a new wine, a
Sauvignon Blanc from the Napa Valley in
California. In the background, the radio was
playing a familiar piano melody, Debussy's
Claire de Lune.

"I do find it most relaxing after a stressful
day at the hospital", said Dr. Moreau.

"My God," exclaimed Nick.
"I remember now!"

"It was played at a concert in a vineyard
in Napa, when I was with a lovely girl from
San Francisco named Laura. No, not Laura
. . . it was . . . Louise! Louise Linden, she
was an airline stewardess with United. It's all
coming back to me now. We spent a few days
together touring the vineyards and she asked
me to accompany her to her friend's wedding

in Hawaii. It all ties in with the information sent to me by Townsend. No wonder the luau last night jogged my memory. And this wine, we first tasted it together in Napa at the very winery on your bottle's label—the Mondavi Winery. That is where we fell in love, I believe. And the wedding," cried Nick, "that is definitely what cemented our relationship."

Dr. Moreau was nearly as excited as Nick and he emptied the remains of the bottle into their glasses, raising his in a toast to his young friend. Nick babbled on about the wedding, much to the joy and amusement of the good doctor.

"Now, mon ami, I think it is time for you to put your life back together," he said. Nick could not agree more, and he thanked his host profusely.

Nick could not wait to give Bruce the good news and make plans to leave Tahiti on his quest for the passport to his future homecoming. But first, he would write to Louise in San Francisco. The only address he remembered was that of United, to whom he wrote, with a request to forward his message

to Louise personally. He ruefully explained
what had happened to him during the past two
years, hoping fervently that she would still be
there for him.

Meanwhile, Bruce came up with an
interesting suggestion. Knowing that Nick was
short on funds, he introduced him to a cruise
ship captain in the hope that he might provide
Nick with passage to New Zealand. The young
Spanish captain, Manuel da Costa, joined them
for lunch while his cruise ship was next in port.
He listened sympathetically to Nick's story
and background.

The cruise ship made frequent trips around
the Marquesas Islands, en route to Auckland.
The captain felt sure that Nick would be an
asset to the cruise director on an upcoming
voyage, making particular note of Nick's
talents for drawing and painting. Admitting
that his plan was somewhat unorthodox, and
not quite legal, he laughingly said, "What the
Greek owners of my ship do not know will
not hurt them."

Bruce and Nick were delighted, and a date
was set for Nick to embark. Bruce then wrote

to the British Consul in Auckland, giving evidence of Nick's history, his involuntary status as a refugee in Tahiti, and—having now recovered from his amnesia—his desire to obtain a passport and return to his native land, where his old job awaited him.

Nick was confused and disappointed to receive a brief letter from United in San Francisco stating that their former employee, Louise Linden, had resigned her position over a year ago. They regretted to inform him that she had left no forwarding address.

Nick vowed to pursue his inquiries further and leave no stone unturned in his quest to reunite with Louise.

A month later, the cruise ship returned to Papeete. Following a big celebration tinged with much regret to see him leave, Bruce, Dr. Moreau, and several of Nick's friends bid him a fond farewell with good wishes for his future and the hope that some day he would return to visit them. Nick thanked his friends deeply for saving his life and for their kind friendship, promising that indeed he would return one day, hopefully with his bride.

CHAPTER TEN

The twelve-day cruise was a delightful
experience, with Nick doing everything
possible to assist in whatever duties he could
to compensate his hosts for the free passage.
Apart from assisting the cruise director, he
arranged with the chef to demonstrate to the
passengers the correct method of making
a real Yorkshire pudding. He delighted in
visiting the islands of Bora Bora, Raiatea, and
Rarotonga, regretting only that the ship could
not call at Manihi, where he so wished to
thank his original rescuers.

Upon arrival in Auckland, he was greeted
by a representative of the British Consulate
where, thanks to Bruce's evidentiary
correspondence, he was granted a temporary

visa while they contacted the British authorities in the U.K. for the issue of an official passport. There was still a problem of a place to live while waiting, but the assistant consul, himself a budding artist, offered Nick a tiny studio above the garage of his home in an Auckland suburb near the waterfront. Nick was not allowed to work officially, but a blind eye was turned to allow him to set up a mobile easel on which he displayed and sold his paintings. In return, Nick revealed his bowling strength and was invited to play cricket with the local team for the next couple of weeks.

Townsend sent him an advance expense check to cover his flight home and urged him to make his delayed report on the budding wineries. Renting a car, he drove the quiet roads to Hawkes Bay, and later to the Marlborough area on the tip of South Island across the bay from Wellington. Within a week, he was able to visit several vineyard wineries where the combination of soil and climate, combined with the dedicated skill of the winemakers, was producing very

promising vintages—both red and white,
and especially the blend of Sauvignon Blanc.
He felt sure that, with an infusion of much
needed capital, these wineries could produce a
quality to rival the best in the world.

Checking his original passport details, the
authorities in the U.K. issued instructions
for their New Zealand Consulate to issue a
new passport for Nicholas Summers and so,
with great relief, Nick managed to arrange a
flight which allowed him to change planes in
San Francisco before continuing to London.
Hopefully the few hours layover would
enable him to search further for Louise.
With profuse thanks to his Kiwi hosts, Nick
produced his best bowling effort and to their
delight, he took five wickets for only 36 runs.
They gave him a rousing round of applause
and a celebration victory party to send him
on his way.

This time, the weather across the Pacific was
calm. He was handed a glass of champagne
by the attractive blonde, blue-eyed flight
attendant (who, in Nick's imagination,
reminded him of Louise) along with an in-

flight magazine before she took his order for dinner. Leafing idly through the magazine, Nick came to the center spread, which heralded "The Paradise of the Pacific" in colorful detail, extolling the splendor of the Coco Palms Resort in Kauai. There, staring out at him, was the smiling face of their star entertainer, Kimo. The entire wedding scene came vividly into Nick's mind as he realized that surely Kimo and his bride Malia would know of Louise's whereabouts.

As the flight hours slipped by, he could not sleep for the excitement the magazine article had generated. He now felt encouraged that his quest would be successful. The plane would not be stopping in Honolulu, but he would write to them as soon as possible in the event that his inquiries in San Francisco did not prove fruitful.

In the few hours he spent in San Francisco, Nick tried once again to question United, hoping that perhaps one or more of their personnel would know something about Louise following her resignation. He checked for her listing in the local telephone directory,

which produced only an automatic response
that the number had been disconnected.
Bitterly disappointed, he continued on his
homebound journey to London to pick
up the life he had left behind over 18
months ago.

CHAPTER ELEVEN

Arriving on a chilly December morning in London, he received a joyful reception at the Townsend office and learned they had managed to release him from his apartment rental agreement after the news of his apparent demise, and removed his personal belongings, sending them to his family in Yorkshire. Nick found a small bed-sitter in the Bloomsbury area, with a convenient connection by underground to the Townsend office at St. Paul's. On the approaching Christmas weekend, his first weekend off work, he rented a small van and drove up to Yorkshire to visit his family and to retrieve some much needed winter clothing. For the best part of two years he had lived in the tropics, apart from the relatively mild period in New Zealand.

Tears of joy greeted him in the family
home in Wombwell, as they listened in virtual
disbelief at his recounting of his adventures.
Local friends stopped by to welcome
Nick home as the family gathered for the
traditional Christmas dinner of roast goose,
mince pies, and plum pudding. Christmas
presents were exchanged all around,
a Tahitian doll delighting Daisy's
infant daughter.

Nick had not known what to bring for the
rest of the family, but he had purchased silk
scarves for the ladies, and a huge box of
chocolates for everyone to enjoy.

Wrapping himself in his winter clothes, he
and Jo took long walks across the windswept
moors. Jo informed him that the Trust which
had been set up for him from the wills of his
parents and grandparents, and which had seen
him through his youth and college education,
was dormant, but still administered by an
aging solicitor in Barnsley. She would arrange
to terminate the Trust and have the proceeds
deposited in Nick's own bank account.

He had forgotten that there might still be money available to him from this and was grateful that it would now give him a start in his new life.

Packing his few personal belongings and clothes into the van, Nick returned to London and contacted the manager of his former apartment building, where he was fortunate to find a pleasant vacant unit available in January. With a soon-to-be replenished bank account, Nick was ready to resume a comfortable life in London.

There was little work to be done in the Townsend office between Christmas and New Year's, on the eve of which Nick was pleased to be invited to a party given by Terry Crawford, one of his more affluent co-workers. Entering the brightly lit and decorated living room of Terry's flat overlooking the Thames, he did not anticipate that fate would now steer him in an entirely new direction.

His attention was drawn to an attractive young woman, surrounded by admirers, all toasting each other with champagne.

She was of medium height and slim build, with wavy brown hair, highlighted by reddish tints. Her dark brown eyes penetrated luminously from a pale oval face which was carefully, but not overly, made up. She was expensively dressed in what Nick imagined was a designer dress, and it showed off her neat figure to perfection. A pearl necklace and matching earrings were her only jewels, apart from a gold wristwatch and a topaz cocktail ring. In a room full of attractive females, she managed to command the attention of most of the men present with her vibrant personality and peals of laughter.

Nick waited for an opening opportunity, and moved to her side with an offer to replenish her glass of champagne.

"Thank you, kind sir," she said coyly, "and who might you be, may I ask?"

"Oh, I'm just one of the guys at Townsend," replied Nick airily. "Terry and I work in the same department."

"Strange, then, that I don't recall seeing you before. Terry and I are old friends, and he is the quintessential party-giver."

"Well, I've been away overseas for awhile. It's good to be back, though. Allow me to introduce myself. I am Nick Summers."

"Good Heavens, you are the fellow who was missing from that awful air crash in the Pacific a couple of years ago. Welcome back to the land of the living. I am Julia Winthrop, by the way," and she proffered her hand, which Nick kissed in a cavalier manner.

"Look," said Julia, "I have to get out of here. I have an early morning business appointment."

"On New Year's Day?" questioned Nick with surprise.

"Yes," said Julia, "it's a special winter shoot in Hyde Park. I'm the fashion editor for Style magazine. Here's my card. Give me a call next week and you can tell me all about your adventures over lunch."

With that parting remark, Julia ran over and kissed her host, Terry, on the cheek, waving to everyone in the room and to no one in particular. With that she was off, leaving Nick staring after her with a mixture of mild amusement and curiosity. He pocketed her card and went over to bid his host farewell.

"Interesting young lady," he said to Terry.

"Oh, indeed," replied Terry "Go for it, she'd be good for you. Cheer you up. Just what you need, old chap."

"Oh," said Nick, surprised, "you and she are not…?"

"Not at all," said Terry. "She and I are like an old brother-sister act."

"Well," said Nick, "it's just lunch."

Nick went back to his rather dreary bed-sitter and prepared to move into his new lodgings next day. New Year's Day dawned cold and bright. Nick wondered how Julia was faring with her fashion models in Hyde Park. He resisted the temptation to stroll over there from his new Knightsbridge location and instead popped in to a nearby pub for brunch and a little inconsequential chit-chat. He retired early that evening and fell into a deep sleep with confusing dreams about chasing after a misty figure through a tropical forest, who eluded capture and eventually drifted up into the clouds.

Waking up thirsty in the pre-dawn hours,

he decided to brave the cold and go for a
run in the park. Hopefully that would help
clear his head and vanquish the after effects
of too much champagne. A hearty breakfast
seemed to be the order of the day and he
found solace in a nearby cafe with a plate of
eggs, bacon, and sausage, followed by a gallon
of strong black coffee. Perusing the morning
paper, he turned to the travel section, full of
tempting ads for winter escapes to tropical
climes. He suddenly realized he had forgotten
to write to Kimo and Malia and sat down
to wish them belated New Year greetings,
plus a request for any knowledge of Louise.
Having no personal address for them, he
mailed his letter to Kimo at the Coco Palms
resort, taking care to inform them of his long
recuperation and rehabilitation following the
airplane disaster and his subsequent search
for Louise.

CHAPTER TWELVE

With the holidays behind him, Nick turned his attention to the myriad of schemes awaiting his attention at the Townsend office. He was assigned to investigate projects in Holland, Germany, and France in the field of electronic technology, making frequent trips by hovercraft across the channel. Some of these research projects would never get off the ground, while others promised rich rewards for those investors willing to take calculated risks. Nick's research was vital to the interests of Townsend's investor clients, and as his expertise increased, he became a rising star in the company. He even made one or two modest investments of his own, achieving some success for his astute judgment.

Crocuses began sprouting up in the parks, heralding an early spring as Nick devoted himself diligently to his work, leaving him scant time for social activity. He received a reply to his letter to Kimo and Malia with both good news and bad news. The good news was the announcement of the birth of healthy twin girls to the young couple. The bad news was that they had completely lost touch with Louise. They knew only that she had left her job at United, and had apparently also left San Francisco, leaving no forwarding address.

They were astonished to learn what had happened to Nick as they had, with everyone else, assumed he did not survive the crash. They added that Louise had been devastated too, and was very depressed the last time they saw her. None of her fellow flight attendants were able to give Malia any news of her whereabouts. Nick was non-plussed to receive this news, which he shared with Jo up in Yorkshire.

"You must make a new life for yourself, my

dear boy," she advised. With typical Yorkshire
stoicism, she added, "What is meant to
be, will be." Nick did not find this very
comforting, though he was forced to accept
her wisdom.

His office phone rang one day in late
February with a call from Julia.

"You never called, you naughty man,"
she chided.

"Have you been off again on one of
your adventures?"

"Not one big adventure," replied Nick, "but
lots of little ones. 'Mea culpa', but enough of
apologies. Let's meet for lunch one day next
week, whenever you are free."

They made a date for Sunday brunch at a
newly opened cafe along the Serpentine in
Hyde Park, hoping for a mild morning and
keeping the date as informal as possible. Luck
with the notoriously fickle English weather
smiled upon them, as they enjoyed a simple
meal and a leisurely stroll along Park Lane.

"Care for a movie?" ventured Nick, and
they agreed to see a matinee performance of
a new French movie at the Curzon Cinema, a

small but luxurious theatre in Mayfair.

"Your call," said Julia, "but I hope there are sub-titles."

"Not to worry," said Nick, "I'm sure there will be, and if not, I'll be happy to fill in the details afterwards over tea at Gunter's."

"Fabulous," cried Julia. "Gunter's is my favorite teashop. I just love their yummy pastries."

Their casual Sunday brunch date turned into a very full and satisfying all-day outing, as tea at Gunter's was followed by a farewell supper at The Three Horseguards, a popular Knightsbridge pub with a new gourmet chef. Conversation with Julia was so easy and free-flowing, they learned of each other's mutual tastes in art, music, and theater. Julia described her career as editor of the fashion magazine, which often took her to exotic locations for fashion shoots, while Nick did his best to explain the mysteries of high finance, which often took him to interesting, if not so exotic locations. Clearly, travel was a key part of both their agendas.

At the end of the day, they agreed to meet

again soon. "Next time," promised Nick, "I will remember to call you and, providing I am not gallivanting around the continent, perhaps we can do a London theatre or concert."

With these parting remarks, he escorted her back to her Chelsea apartment. They kissed each other good night—a perfunctory peck on the cheek—and she thanked him for a delightful day, but did not ask him up for the proverbial nightcap.

"Thank God," thought Nick, silently. "This is moving a bit too fast."

Nevertheless, he admitted to himself that it had been a wonderful day, and a sense of courtesy told him he should call and tell her so the next morning. She received his call with obvious pleasure, telling him she had to dash off to Hollywood the next week to do a feature article for the magazine about the Academy Awards.

"I'll be back for Easter," she told him, and Nick was relieved that the pressure was off for a quick follow-up date.

"Bon Voyage," he wished her. "I'd love to hear all about the Oscar ceremonies and perhaps we can hope for a British win this time around."

A month later, Nick called Julia, who apologized for having been overwhelmed by work following her return from California.

"How was it all?" asked Nick. "Oh, absolutely wonderful," replied Julia, "and we celebrated with Glenda Jackson, for her Oscar for *Touch of Class*. If it's showing somewhere I'd love to see it again." And so, a mutually convenient date was agreed upon.

Over a late supper, Nick mentioned a new Broadway musical called *Gypsy* opening soon in the West End, which was receiving a lot of advance publicity.

"Oh, yes," cried Julia. "I'd love to see it, but don't buy tickets. I'm sure to be invited to the opening night and you can be my date. A new musical usually brings out the fashionable social set and I'll need to cover it for my magazine."

"Sounds good," said Nick, "you're a handy girl to know. I'll accept the show tickets, and it will be my treat for supper afterwards, even if you can write it off to expenses."

Enjoying the light banter, Nick was happy to engage in a not too serious relationship. They both enjoyed the same taste in movies, concerts, and theater, which led to several dates over the next few months. Both of them had busy work schedules which helped keep a sensible and reasonable distance between meetings.

One memorable evening was spent at the Royal Albert Hall, where Australian legend Eileen Joyce celebrated the 25th anniversary of her brilliant recording of the Rachmaninoff second piano concerto on the soundtrack of the movie *Brief Encounter*. Both Nick and Julia sat enraptured by the romantic second movement, each reaching for the other's hand in the darkness and thus further cementing a growing infatuation. That New Year's Eve they attended Terry Crawford's annual party, marking the first anniversary of their initial meeting. Swooning slightly from the liberal champagne toasts, they left the party shortly after midnight, strolling arm in arm along the embankment and murmuring, "Your place or mine?"

CHAPTER THIRTEEN

In the year that followed they became constant companions, interrupted only by their respective travel assignments. Julia covered fashionable events such as Ascot, the Derby, Paris Fashion Week—often with Nick in tow. Nick's business assignments took him all over the U.K., from cattle breeding in the Southwest, to oil rig projects in Scotland, as well as frequent trips to the continent.

Desperately needing a vacation, Nick accepted Julia's invitation to attend the Cannes Film Festival. Somewhat bored by the effusive crowds in Cannes, Nick took the opportunity to rent a car and explore the Riviera while Julia fulfilled her obligations. Hopefully, by week's end, they would have a chance to share a restful few days in the sunshine. Meanwhile, Nick explored the

mountain villages outside Cannes, reveling
in the atmosphere of the cobbled alleyways
and ancient archways of St. Paul de Vence,
the village of Mougins, and Picasso's pottery
village of Vallauris. He particularly enjoyed a
visit to the home of Auguste Renoir in nearby
Cagnes. A great admirer of Renoir's paintings
of Provence and its people, Nick was inspired
to take up his own painting hobby again.

Julia joined him at the end of her frantic
week in Cannes, and together they explored
the high mountain village of Eze and a quick
trip to the casino in Beaulieu. Monte Carlo
beckoned, but would have to wait. Instead,
they opted for a more relaxed experience as
they checked in to the refined elegance of
the Hotel Royal at the entrance to Cap Ferrat
where, between sunbathing and swimming,
Julia had a few unhurried hours to write up
her experiences at the Cannes Festival.

In shorts and espadrilles, they strolled along
the sea wall to the charming little port of
St. Jean for a lazy lunch, eschewing the lure
of the casinos in favor of relaxed outdoor
dinners on the hotel terrace, and early nights.

Nick was relieved that Julia made no demands
on him and appeared to be quite content
with their comfortable relationship. He still
thought about Louise, realizing how great
was the difference between his ardent feelings
for her and his current friendship with Julia.
Sometimes he dreamed that one day Louise
would miraculously come back into his life.

CHAPTER FOURTEEN

Back in London and feeling considerably refreshed, Nick was introduced to an important client of Townsend, a French banker and businessman, Monsieur Pierre Duval. He owned a couple of small vineyards in the Loire and Dordogne valleys, and he had expressed to Townsend that he was interested in the new developments in the California wine industry. He was aware that, in a recent number of tastings in the United States, the California wines had earned high praise, though they faced difficulty in marketing their product, possibly due to the public's preference for the so-called "superior" French wines.

Townsend mentioned Nick's experience in the Napa Valley region and suggested that he and Duval share their knowledge. Nick knew that the glowing accounts of the U.S. wine tastings in the early 1970s had been largely discounted by most European experts as somewhat biased and presumptive, often claiming that the French wines had possibly suffered in transit. Duval had already traveled to California on a fact-finding trip to several Napa Valley wineries and had been impressed by the innovations in the fertilizing, cultivating, and production methods they employed. He was interested to learn from them and sought advice on investment possibilities. Unlike many of his peers in France, Duval kept an open mind regarding the quality of the California product. Aware also that the Americans were experiencing skepticism among potential investors, he worked closely with Nick to find the right opportunities.

In 1976, a remarkable wine event was organized by a British wine merchant, whose own wine school was actually based in Paris. Determined to prove the superiority of the French wines, he set up a panel of French wine-tasting experts to judge the California vintages against their French counterparts. Dubbed "The Judgment of Paris," the event was covered by the international press to prove once and for all to the entire world, the superiority of French wines. In the elaborate blind tasting which followed, everyone— especially the undoubtedly prejudiced French judges—failed to recognize their own French favorites and, to everyone's astonishment, pronounced a California Chardonnay the winner, with two other California vineyards taking third and fourth place. In the red category, the top three were all from Napa, beating out the venerable and highly respected Chateau Mouton Rothschild into fourth place.

As a Frenchman, Duval was embarrassed. But as an astute businessman, he was determined to pursue his investments in the Napa Valley, and Nick set up a series of appointments for him during the month of August, a period when most Frenchmen put aside their business activities in favor of family vacations in Provence. Duval decided to take his wife and six-year-old daughter to California instead. To amuse their daughter, they first visited Disneyland, then drove up the coast road via Santa Barbara and Hearst Castle to San Francisco. Riding the cable car to Fisherman's Wharf was an exciting treat for the whole family, and Duval apologized that following their sightseeing, he would have to drive up to the Napa Valley to check up on his vineyard investments. "Not so much fun for a little girl," he admitted, "but you and Maman can relax at a spa and play some tennis and swim, while Papa goes about his business." So saying, he checked the family into the Silverado Resort.

On a visit to a consortium of small Napa wineries, Duval was introduced to Louise Linden working as assistant to the Director. He was impressed with her charm and ability to deal with people, as well as her office skills and knowledge of the wine industry. Spying a photograph on her desk of a smiling little girl about the same age as his daughter Lilli, he learned that it was of her daughter Jenny.

"Would you care to visit my wife and daughter at the Silverado Resort?" he asked. "I'm sure the two little girls would enjoy playing together for the day next Sunday." At the mention of Silverado, Louise tried hard to stifle back a tear as her mind wandered back to the time she had spent there with Nick. However, she did not wish to disappoint the charming Frenchman, or her daughter's chance of a new playmate.

"Well, Sunday is our busiest day up here," replied Louise, "with many visitors to the tasting rooms. But I could drop Jenny off in the morning and introduce her to your daughter."

"Parfait," replied the Frenchman, "they can play together while you and I do the business, and you must certainly join us all for dinner that evening."

The two children met and enjoyed a delightful day together under the watchful eye of Helene Duval. Jenny did not speak French, but Lilli was already learning English, in common with all the children in her French lycée. With a few phrases and many gestures, they played jump rope, swam, and frolicked together. Over the next two weeks, it became clear that the two girls had bonded and become good playmates. Duval shrewdly observed how well Louise performed her job with the consortium, assisting in the tasting rooms, smoothly running the office, arranging special events, and conducting educational tours of the vineyards for visiting tourists.

As the time for departure drew near, Duval had an inspiration.

"You know, Louise," he said, "I wish I had someone like you to assist me with my wineries and general business affairs in France. Our children adore each other, my wife and I greatly admire you. Is there any chance you would consider coming to work for me?"

"In France?" asked Louise incredulously.

"Mais oui," declared the Frenchman, "bien sur. I see you are surprised, but perhaps you would like to think about it. I shall return in about six months, and I hope you will give it every consideration. As for your little girl, I am sure I can enroll her in the same

lycée with Lilli, where she will have a good
education. She has already picked up several
French phrases and the school has a special
course for foreign students. I never told you,"
he continued, "how much Lilli misses her
twin sister, whom we sadly lost a couple of
years ago."

All of this came as quite a shock to Louise,
as she bid farewell to the amiable Frenchman
and his wife. Her head was in a whirl. Could
she seriously contemplate such a dramatic
change in her lifestyle? Aunt Grace and Uncle
George had been so kind to her and Jenny,
but they were aging and not in the best of
health. Without them, she would be alone in
the world, her mother having passed away—
in fact, everyone she ever cared for had gone.
Louise did speak passable French, as one of
the requirements in her former airline job
was reasonable fluency in at least one foreign
language. Jenny was young and eager to learn.
Duval could be very persuasive, and his offer
of a home, employment, and schooling for
Jenny was an intriguing proposition. He was
so kind and understanding, giving her time

to think it over, and this she proceeded to do until his next visit.

By the following spring, she had decided to take the plunge. Aunt Grace and Uncle George were very understanding and, while not exactly encouraging her, neither did they stand in her way. Duval was delighted with her decision and made all the necessary arrangements for travel and a work permit, as well as accommodation in a cottage on the grounds of his villa in Barbizon, just 30 minutes drive from the center of Paris, to which he commuted daily. He was already in the process of transferring the bulk of his business affairs to his home, where Louise would work, close to her daughter's school.

The transition went smoothly and shortly after Easter, Jenny was celebrating her seventh birthday with Lilli and half a dozen school friends. Duval hired a young English governess, Nanette, who was bi-lingual—her English father having met her French mother while serving during the war in Normandy. She soon endeared herself to the entire family.

Louise visited Duval's wineries in the Loire Valley and in the Dordogne, discreetly adding some American flair to their activities. She handled the business affairs with a newfound confidence and felt happy and secure for the first time in many years. The town of Barbizon was an idyllic haven on the outskirts of the forest of Fontainebleau, housing the Barbizon School of Painting that focused on the 19th-century art movement called "Realism" or "Naturalist." Its original inspiration came from the English painter John Constable, though later artists such as Millet and Rousseau had added a touch of realism to their works with their inclusion of the everyday workers who inhabited their landscapes. Louise became infatuated with the quaint little tourist town with its museum, galleries, and art workshops dedicated to its artistic past. She was also surprised to find that Duval's business interests were by no means limited to his wineries. He owned a wine store and tasting room in Barbizon itself, and his widespread investments included spare parts and electronics plants in Toulouse, associated with the rapidly expanding aircraft industry.

The man was a veritable dynamo and kept Louise busy adapting to his varied businesses. As tireless as he appeared to be, Duval was beginning to show signs of increased stress and fatigue. Having married rather late in life, he was of an entirely different generation, and his efforts to discipline his daughter were superseded by his affection for her. As an 18-year-old, he had fled his native country to join the Free French forces in England, and thus had an abiding affection for his neighbor across the channel, which made for an easy relationship with Nick and his investment advisors at the Townsend Company.

CHAPTER FIFTEEN

Although his business relationship with
Nick was entirely professional, Duval had
developed a fondness for the younger man,
which resulted in his extending an invitation
to visit him and his family in his Barbizon
home for Le Quatorze Juillet, the big summer
festival celebrating France's liberty. Nick was
flattered and readily accepted, noting that
Julia was going to be out of town for the
week. He flew over a day earlier to enjoy the
artistic delights of the painter's village and
was welcomed by Duval declaring, "Don't
forget your paintbrush, Nick. We will feast
and enjoy our wines and we will not discuss
the business affairs." Secretly he wondered
how Nick and Louise would get along, totally

unaware of their meeting a decade earlier. He fancied himself a good judge of character and personalities and took more than a little pleasure in attempting to play Cupid. When Nick entered the living room of the villa, he was greeted by Duval's wife, Helene.

"Vous etes bien venue, Monsieur. Make yourself at home and enjoy a glass of my husband's favorite Sancerre from his own vineyard in the Loire. The girls will be back shortly. They have been shopping in the village for delicacies for our Bastille Day Eve dinner tonight."

Nick wandered out to the terrace to sip his wine and admire the beautifully tended garden. Soon he was attracted by the sound of children's laughter and the voice of their English nanny from the room within. "Be good and practice your piano lessons while I take these baskets to the kitchen," she said. Nick was soon entranced by the strains of music floating out to the terrace. The two girls were seated at the piano, one of them playing softly while the other turned the music pages. The haunting melody that reached him was something he had heard before. Debussy's *Claire de Lune*.

Too polite to interrupt, he waited outside the room before entering and introducing himself. As he advanced towards the piano, he was struck in particular by the sight of one of the girls, with long blonde curls tied back with a blue ribbon, and the bluest eyes he had seen since . . . . His thoughts flashed momentarily back to his long lost Louise. The resemblance was striking.

"Hello," he said, "I am your Papa's friend, Nick. I suppose you two are his daughters?"

"Not exactly," said the darker of the two. "I am Lilli Duval, and this is my very best friend, Jenny Linden. We are almost like sisters, though. Do you play the piano?"

"No, said Nick, but I love hearing that piece you were playing. Don't stop because of me. I'll just sit over there in the corner and listen."

"Thank you, Monsieur," said Lilli, and the girls resumed their seats at the piano.

The name Linden startled Nick, as he retreated to the shadow of the corner armchair. He was equally startled by the resemblance of the child to Louise. He sat enchanted as Jenny played and Lilli assisted her. The delicate features, the hair, and the eyes were unmistakable. Could this be Louise's child?

As he watched and reflected, he suddenly became aware of a figure in a summery white dress, standing in the open French window, her face partly in shadow, and her hair backlit by the rays of the setting sun. He rose to his feet, transfixed by the sight of Louise as she entered the room and greeted the girls at the piano. Suddenly aware of his presence in the corner of the room, Louise was equally transfixed.

Covering her mouth with the back of her hand, she gasped and murmured, "My God, am I seeing a ghost or is this really you? I thought . . ." She could not complete the sentence, as she stared at Nick in astonishment.

"Yes, it is indeed me," said Nick, his arm outstretched as she appeared to falter. "Louise, my dearest Louise, I have so longed to find you again."

Pointing to the two girls engrossed at the piano, Louise raised her fingers to her lips and ushered Nick out onto the terrace.

"I cannot believe this is really happening," she said. "You disappeared completely out of my life so long ago, and now you suddenly show up?"

"Please, my dearest, we need to talk and I will explain everything," said Nick.

"I cannot imagine," began Louise, "but this is not the time or the place. The children would not understand—we must be very discreet, and yes, I certainly would like you to explain."

Nick detected a coolness in Louise which was unlike her, and he realized the difficulty of the situation. The Duvals had no idea that they had met more than a decade ago, and explanations were needed all around.

"I am very puzzled," said Louise, "but of course we need to talk alone. We cannot just spring this on the entire family. Soon we shall all be sitting round the table together, and I beg you to keep up the pretense of strangers meeting for the first time."

"You don't seem overjoyed to see me," said Nick.

"No, it is not that," replied Louise. "Of course I am delighted to see you, though I do not understand what happened to you. I was devastated to learn of the plane crash and the reports of no survivors. Why on Earth didn't you contact me?"

"Louise, my darling, I realize what a shock this is, for me to show up here after ten years. I searched everywhere for you, too, but nobody knew where you were. OK, I agree we have to play this carefully, and I promise you that when you hear what happened to me you will understand. For now, just know that I love you, have always loved you, and now that fate has brought us together again, there must be a happy ending."

"Oh, Nick, I am so confused, I don't know what to say."

At that moment Duval entered the terrace and said, "Bon. I am glad you two have met. I will bring more wine and we will dispense with the formal introductions and get ready for the superb dinner Helene is preparing.

Tomorrow is the Quatorze Juillet, the day that all France celebrates the storming of the Bastille, and we shall go and join the dancing and the excitement in our little village. Now, excusez-moi, I will get the wine and drink a toast to your new friendship."

With that, Duval turned and left the couple to contemplate how they would play out their charade.

"The little girl, Jenny, at the piano, she bears such a striking resemblance to you, Louise," said Nick as soon as they were alone.

"Not surprising. She is after all, my daughter, and that is my part of the story you will hear later when we are truly alone," said Louise, mysteriously.

Nick's thoughts went instantly back to their love tryst on the beach in Hawaii and, mentally doing the math, he blurted out, "You mean she is actually—"

"Shh," murmured Louise, "Later, my dear, later . . ."

They were soon swept up with the exuberant children and the jolliness of Duval and his wife as they were called to

the dinner table. Assisted by ample pourings
of Duval's favorite wines, about which he
waxed with Gallic eloquence, the gaiety of the
evening helped to mask the turbulent feelings
experienced by Nick and Louise. Finally,
it was time to retire and the couple agreed
to take a stroll in the nearby woods next
morning, where each could reveal their inner
thoughts and secrets.

CHAPTER SIXTEEN

The next morning, they strolled over to the nearby woods where they could be alone.

"First," began Nick, "I must tell you that after the ghastly crash, I was somehow found floating in the water in my life jacket and miraculously rescued by some fishermen, who took me to their little island—not even an island, just a tiny, sparsely populated atoll in the middle of the ocean, called Manihi. I was barely conscious, suffering from shock and exposure, and spent many days in a coma while they kindly tended to my injuries. When I finally awoke, I was still in a complete daze. I had no memory of who I was and what had happened. It was case of total amnesia."

Louise looked at him with horror. "Go

on," she said, with sympathy in her voice. Nick continued to relate that much time had elapsed as he gathered strength until his diving accident, which led to his being transferred to the hospital in Papeete. She listened attentively as he recounted his treatment under Dr. Moreau and his fortuitous introduction to Bruce, a fellow graduate of Cambridge whose old alumni magazines had helped to reveal his true identity.

"How incredibly fortunate you were to have so much care from the doctor and the consul" said Louise. "What an amazing coincidence that you met Bruce. I could not have imagined such a miracle, but please, go on."

"There's so much more to tell you," said Nick, "but first you must know that once I recovered, and more than a year had gone by, I made extensive inquiries after you, only to find that you had resigned from the airline and no one, not even Malia, knew where you were or how to find you. I did not know where to turn. What made you cut off all your ties and literally disappear?"

"Now it's my turn," replied Louise. "When I heard of the crash with no survivors, I was devastated. I checked with the airline and reread the news reports. It seemed that no one had survived. My last memory of you was in Kauai, when I awoke at dawn and found you sleeping soundly. The previous night was the happiest and most wonderful experience of my life. I was so anxious to talk to you, but I had to resume my schedule with an early flight back to San Francisco. I thought it best to leave you sleeping, and so I left you a note, knowing you would soon be on your way to New Zealand, and not knowing when we would be together again, but hoping fervently that there would be a future for us.

I returned to work, but I was very depressed. My mother was dying of ovarian cancer. I thought you were dead and with it my hopes for a happy future. I could not concentrate—it was not easy to be cheerful to my passengers when I was feeling sick and utterly miserable. I tried to do my job, but I could not sleep and I was feeling nauseous. At first I put it down to depression, but later on my doctor told me I was pregnant and the constant flights back and forth were not helping. I realized I could not continue and so I resigned before my condition became obvious. I wanted to get away from my friends and everyone who knew me, so I went to my aunt and uncle in Vallejo. Yes, Nick, it was that wonderful night on the beach—of course Jenny is my, our daughter."

Louise continued to relate her life with her aunt and uncle, how welcome they made her and how much happiness Jenny had brought into all their lives, leading up to the job in Napa and her meeting years later with Pierre Duval. "The rest you know."

"And for years I have worked with Duval," said Nick. "How could we have known that he was the one destined to bring us back together?"

"Does it matter?" asked Louise, "I bless his heart for thinking so kindly of us. I'm so sorry, Nick, for all the years we have wasted. I realize I should have left a forwarding address

when I left San Francisco. When I thought
you had died, my life lost its meaning. Then
when Jenny arrived, I learned to live again.
If I had not gone to Vallejo I might never
have worked in Napa, and never have met
Duval. Little did I know that he would be the
architect of our reunion."

Tears welled in Louise's eyes, as Nick
embraced her closely. "Nothing matters any
more, my darling. Now that we have found
each other, I never want to let you go. Jenny
is adorable and I want to take care of both of
you so that we can finally be a family."

"You really mean that?" asked Louise.

"I certainly do," said Nick.

"But Nick dear, we just cannot rush into
this. I have to choose the right moment to
explain everything to Jenny, not the least to
how we break the news to the Duvals. I think
we must keep up the pretense until Jenny
understands our secret. Then we shall have
to tell the Duvals how we met years ago and
would have married had it not been for your
supposed death in the airline crash
and your rescue in Tahiti and the amnesia

which followed."

"Whatever it takes, darling, I'll play it any way you want it, as long as you agree to the outcome," said Nick.

"And that would be . . . ?"

"Louise, my angel, do I have to get down and soil my knees on this forest floor in order to propose to you? I think we both deserve a second chance. . . . ?"

"What a great idea," said Louise, ". . . and I accept."

They agreed that out of courtesy to the Duvals, they should first reveal their secret to the kindly couple, asking them for more time for the best way to approach Jenny. Bastille Day was warm and sunny, the whole family enjoyed the parade, the picnic and the evening fireworks. The children were happy and so tired they practically fell into bed, leaving Nick and Louise to explain their relationship and Jenny's birth to the sympathetic couple.

"We are so happy for you both," said Duval, "and I am the most happy man for bringing you together."

Nick delayed his return to London for

another day in order to spend it in private
with Louise and Jenny. Louise suggested that
she first take Jenny up to her bedroom and
look at the only photograph she had of Nick,
taken together with Malia and Kimo at their
wedding. Nick was barely recognizable in his
straw hat and dark sunglasses, but Louise had
always told Jenny that he was her father,
who had died in an airplane crash before
she was born.

Looking at the photograph now with Jenny,
Louise began the long explanation of Nick's
rescue, unknown to her at the time, and the
meaning of the amnesia which had kept him
away so long.

"We loved each other very much, dear, and
we just did not have enough time to make our
own wedding arrangements, until after your
daddy returned from New Zealand. I thought
we had lost him forever, until very recently
when I found out that he was alive and well.
For years he has tried to reach me, but could
not do so as I had left my hometown.
He never knew about you until now."

Jenny gazed at the photo in perplexed

amazement. "Do you mean he has come back to us?" asked Jenny, her eyes wide and her lips trembling.

"Yes, my darling, you met him yesterday."

"The English gentleman?" asked Jenny. "He seems very nice."

"He is waiting for us downstairs in the garden," said Louise. "I am sure you will have lots of questions, but let me assure you, my darling—we are going to be a real family now."

"Will you get married properly, then?" asked Jenny.

"Yes, my darling, just as soon as we can make the necessary arrangements, and you will be our very special bridesmaid."

"Lilli too?"

"Why of course," replied Louise, hugging her child closely. "It will be a wonderful celebration for all of us."

Jenny ran downstairs to the garden terrace, where Nick embraced her warmly, delighted that she was so eager to accept him.

"I am so happy, today," said Nick, "but tomorrow I must return to London for a little while to attend to my business affairs. I will return as soon as I can get away, and now that we have found each other, I never want us to be apart again. Now we have to go and find Lilli and tell her the good news."

"What about Monsieur and Madame Duval?" Jenny asked.

"Yes, we have told them," said Nick, "and tonight we will all celebrate together."

He decided that for now he would ignore the proverbial "elephant in the room," namely his relationship with Julia Winthrop. That would be the next big problem he was determined to deal with on his return to London.

CHAPTER SEVENTEEN

As events transpired, he was greeted by Bill Townsend, who told him he was about to retire and that he was arranging for his company to be merged with the powerful Barclays group.

"They have agreed to take in all of our key personnel," said Townsend, assuring Nick of his continued employment. Nick congratulated Townsend on his retirement, but said nothing more. He had never cared for the executives at the huge banking firm, and could not envision himself working within their empire. Though he was not yet ready to admit it, he saw his escape route lying before him.

He now faced the hurdle of breaking his

news to Julia. "Julia, my dear," he began, when calling her for their usual Sunday pub lunch, "we need to talk."

"Of course," she said, "I hope you enjoyed your little trip to France. Did everything go well?"

"Everything was fine," answered Nick, "but that's not what I want to talk to you about."

"Well," replied Julia, "you look so serious, but I am afraid it will have to wait. I am off to Milan early tomorrow morning for the fashion show and then on to Venice to cover the Film Festival."

Nick was used to her rather abrupt manner when she was busy preparing for a major event. Her business career was always her number one priority.

"Yes," said Nick, "we always seem to be off in different directions."

If Julia detected a sour note, she did not show it. Instead she babbled on about the demands on her time.

"Townsend is retiring," Nick told her, "and I am thinking of making a move myself. I hope to have news for you when you return from Italy."

"Marvelous" said Julia, "I'm sure you'll make the right decision for your future."

You're darn right, thought Nick silently, and he refrained from making further comment.

"Time," he muttered under his breath, "I just need a little more time."

With Julia away, Nick was in daily contact with Louise, always spending some time on the phone with Jenny. When he told Louise about the situation with Townsend and Barclays, she asked, "What will you do?"

"I will need a little time," he told her, "but you can start looking for a small villa for us in Barbizon. It's a great place to relax, and I am following up some leads," he replied vaguely. "Perhaps you can do a little research with the real estate people."

Louise was so thrilled to hear this, she forgot to ask him how he planned to make a living in Barbizon. Nick had no idea either. He just wanted to assure her that he was making plans for their future together as a family.

Once again, fate took a hand. In Julia's

absence, Nick made a quick trip to France, upset to hear from Helene that her husband was in the hospital, after suffering a mild heart attack brought on by stress.

"He is recovering well," she said, "though the doctors have told him he must slow down. Louise has been merveilleux in handling his business affairs."

Nick visited his friend in the hospital and listened to him sigh with resignation that he would have to plan for an early retirement if he wanted to age gracefully with his wife and see his daughter grow up.

"That makes two of you," said Nick, telling him about Bill Townsend's decision. The Frenchman was thoughtful and asked Nick what his plans were. "I'm desperately trying to find a way to join Louise and Jenny," said Nick. "They love it here, and I am growing fond of the French way of living."

"Let us talk," said Duval. "I am going to need a man with your finesse to help with my affairs, and eventually take over. Louise has been wonderful, but it is too much to expect her to take on more work. Please give it some thought, Nick, and hopefully we can come to some arrangement that will benefit all of us."

Nick was intrigued by the business prospect suggested by Duval. He thanked the Frenchman and wished him a speedy recovery. He and Louise would make an ideal business team, though eventually he had more domesticated plans for her.

Back in London, he turned his attention to Julia. She was a very self-possessed and practical woman, and though their relationship had been close for several years, it was more a friendship of convenience, frequently playing second fiddle to their individual careers and ambitions. Julia returned from Italy, gushing over her detailed report while Nick listened with patient amusement.

Finally, he took the plunge. "Julia, my dear, you are quite a remarkable young woman, and I have thoroughly enjoyed all the fascinating times we have spent together."

"But?" queried Julia, sensing a looming crisis.

"Well," continued Nick, "I thought there was no one I would rather spend time with, but I have a confession to make."

And, with Julia finally wide-eyed and attentive, he related his ten-year history beginning with his first meeting with Louise, the airline disaster, his slow recovery from amnesia in Tahiti, his affair, and fruitless search for Louise.

"When I met you in London," he continued, "I honestly thought that part of my life was over, and that I had lost forever the love of my life. I had to forget her and start over in England. Naturally, that New Year's Eve when we first met, I was attracted by your vibrant personality, and I desperately needed your upbeat company. You breathed new life into me and I don't regret one moment of these past few years."

"What has happened, Nick?" asked Julia with apprehension in her voice. "What else do you have to confess?"

She listened quietly while Nick told her of his chance reunion with Louise in Barbizon, and especially his encounter with Jenny.

"I can understand that you still have feelings for her, but it's the child, isn't it, that's governing your heart? You didn't know you were the father of a ten-year-old, and now you feel your responsibility."

"Yes, of course, Julia, I do feel a great responsibility. But I think I have always loved Louise deep in my heart, and that kind of love doesn't happen twice in a lifetime. A near tragic event parted us, and a miracle has brought us together again."

"So we're through, is that what you are trying to tell me?" asked Julia.

"You were always straightforward, Julia, so I hope you are not bitter."

"No, Nick, I am not bitter," sighed Julia. "I only wish I had not grown so darn fond of you. I know I am not the easiest person on the planet. I only hope we can remain good friends. Marriage and motherhood were never appealing to me, I guess I was always too independent."

"Yes, Julia, I hope we can remain good friends. I admire your forthrightness and your honesty, even though your independent spirit was a bit irksome at times. We had a lot in common and we enjoyed ourselves. There are lots of good times to remember."

"Does she know about us?" asked Julia.

"No," said Nick, "and I don't want to complicate things any further. I know I can trust your discretion. As it happens, I don't expect to spend much time in London in future," and he told her about Townsend's retirement, Duval's offer, and his plan to move to France. "We are going to get married finally and make a home for Jenny."

"As indeed you should," said Julia, "but you know how people talk. She is bound to find out about us sooner or later."

"You're quite right," said Nick. "I don't want to keep any more secrets. I will tell her I have not exactly been a monk all these years."

"If she is half the woman you say she is, she won't expect that you have," replied Julia. "Nick, dear, you know I wish you every happiness and success. Thank you for being so frank with me. Let's have a champagne toast to each other, for friendship's sake."

"For friendship's sake," said Nick, as they clinked glasses.

Returning to his apartment, Nick felt

relieved that a heavy burden had been lifted from his shoulders, and Julia had taken it all with characteristic stoicism. He went into the bathroom and cleared out a few personal toiletries she had left there, reflecting wistfully on the many good times they had enjoyed together. As he stared thoughtfully at his reflection in the mirror, he saw a fit-looking man of 42, with barely the first touch of grey at the temples, a well-traveled man of business experience, and a healthy balance in the bank. Along with some of his clients, he had made a number of astute personal investments. Now a new job and a new life as a family man in another country lay ahead of him, and he felt ready to face the challenges. He was ready once again to move in another direction, this time with a beautiful woman he adored, and a lovely young child by his side.

CHAPTER EIGHTEEN

On the outskirts of Barbizon, Louise had
located a small but attractive villa, close to the
Duval headquarters and to Jenny's school. It
would comfortably house the three of them
and there were additional quarters for guests.
Her doctor had assured her that at 35, she
was healthy and capable of expanding her
little family. She kept this closely in mind as
she began thinking seriously of a wedding
date in the near future. Nick heartily approved
of the villa's location, and Jenny was thrilled
to know she would remain close to her dear
friend Lillli and their school. Duval's offer
to Nick was generous and would allow him
ample time to take over the reins of his
widespread business activities, with Duval

continuing to supervise, but at a slower pace.

Nick and Louise set a wedding date for the following spring, just after Jenny's birthday. Nick was anxious to introduce his newfound family to his adoptive parents in Yorkshire and asked if Louise and Jenny would accompany him to his traditional Christmas holiday with them. A little reluctant to miss the festive Noel season in France, they later readily agreed to make the trip, especially after Louise told her daughter how much Nick owed the kindly Yorkshire folk who had taken him under their wing when he so tragically lost his parents in the wartime bombing raid. Jenny was smart and sensible enough to understand Nick's attachment and gratitude to the wonderful Jo, of whom he had spoken so lovingly.

Christmas in Yorkshire was even colder than Paris and Barbizon, but the warmth and joy extended by the entire Branscombe family more than compensated. Jo was ecstatic to hear of Nick's reunion with Louise and Jenny, and promised to fly over for the wedding. The elder Branscombe had retired from the pits,

suffering from emphysema, but cheerfully
oversaw the family celebration, with his wife
Emily preparing the traditional Christmas
dinner of roast goose, plum pudding, and
mince pies. Jo produced her specialty—a
true Yorkshire pudding, the likes of which
Louise and Jenny had never before tasted,
and which both pronounced as scrumptious.
Jenny played with Daisy's two young children,
and four days passed with much merriment.
Willy gave Jenny a copy of his favorite Brontë
novel, *Jane Eyre*, a story with a young girl as its
heroine, which he thought Jenny would find
particularly appealing.

Nick and family returned to Barbizon
in time for the usual Nouvelle Annee
celebrations with the Duvals and took up
their residence in the new villa. With the
Easter holidays looming, Nick and Louise
decided to have a small wedding ceremony in
the local church, with a reception to follow at
the Duval home. Jenny and Lilli were dressed
in gorgeous pink dresses as bridesmaids, with
Louise beaming serenely in her ivory lace
gown. Jo kept her word and took her first

trip by air outside her home country. The
newlyweds spent their wedding night at the
historic Hotel Du Bas Breau, leaving Jenny to
spend the night with Lilli. They would all stay
in their own villa until Jenny resumed school,
and then take off on a honeymoon trip, the
details of which Nick had so far kept secret.
Jenny was quite happy to stay with Liilli
and the Duvals for the projected month-
long vacation.

Duval's health had improved considerably,
and he assured Nick he could handle
everything during his absence, so Nick felt
able to finally reveal to Louise the careful
plans he had made.

"I thought it would be fun to retrace our
steps," said Nick to his wife, "so I have made
plans accordingly. I do hope you approve."

"I'm all ears," replied Louise. "So tell me all
about it."

"Well," said Nick. "It all began with that
night in Las Vegas, so I thought that is where
we should start." And he began to lay out all
the details of the month-long honeymoon.
"Three nights in Las Vegas, so we can take

in all the sights without rushing, and a nice, comfortable hotel to relax in after our flight from Paris. Then, up to San Francisco where we can pick up a car and drive to Vallejo. I'm sure you will look forward to seeing your aunt and uncle again. Then we can drive up to Napa, take a look at the Duval winery investments, and maybe stop by the Mondavi winery where we so enjoyed that concert."

"Oh, you dear old romantic," interjected Louise. "That's very thoughtful of you. Do go on."

"Well," said Nick, producing a wallet bulging with tickets, brochures, and baggage tags, "from San Francisco, I've booked us on a twelve-day cruise to Tahiti, and it stops over for a day in Hawaii."

"Oh, you darling," cried Louise. "We can see Malia and Kimo and re-live that wonderful wedding experience. I wrote to them from France and told them about our miraculous reunion."

"The ship calls at a couple of islands and winds up in Papeete, where I want you to meet my dear friends and benefactors, Dr.

Moreau and Bruce, and his wife, Tia."

Louise was enchanted and bubbling with excitement. "We have to fly home from there," Nick continued, "and I so wanted to show you the little atoll of Manihi, but there is no airstrip or hotel there." Louise was ecstatic. "It sounds absolutely perfect" she cried, "What a wonderful honeymoon."

"After all we went through," said Nick, "I think we deserve it."

"Oh, my God," said Louise, "I've got to go to Paris and do some shopping."

"That's fine," said Nick, "I'll be tying up some loose ends here. But remember, only two bags—it should be mostly warm weather all the way."

They stayed home until Jenny celebrated her birthday, and then took off for Las Vegas. The spate of new hotels and casinos since their whirlwind tour in the late '60s amazed them. The Strip was virtually transformed into one giant mega resort, with sparkling high rises, a blaze of neon lights, and abundant entertainment. The newly opened Circus Circus provided a spectacle of non-

stop acrobatic thrills, and they re-visited their
original haunts at the Sands and Flamingo,
both now seemingly twice the size they
remembered. For their stay, Nick chose the
Desert Inn since it was so spacious and more
akin to its desert surroundings than the other
hotels with their huge towers. It also boasted
the only hotel golf course in town, which
might provide a daytime escape from the
frantic casino activity.

"In spite of its growth up to now," Nick
said, "there are even more ambitious plans
ahead for this city. I have spoken to a number
of large financial institutions who are
replacing the original investors who built this
city with their dubious sources of capital, and
they will eventually transform the Las Vegas
landscape with some remarkable architectural
achievements, emulating the big sightseeing
attractions of Europe and Asia.

I have heard of plans to build a replica
of the Eiffel Tower, the New York skyline,
Venetian Palaces, and even the Egyptian
Pyramids. The next decade will astonish
everyone. Right now, we can visit the Roman

Coliseum and a typical Roman Piazza
at Caesar's Palace, and you can have fun
shopping in the Forum, while we lunch 'al
fresco' and watch the light change from dawn
to dusk on the artificially painted sky."

"How come you know so much?"
asked Louise.

"It's my business to help people invest in
the future," replied Nick.

CHAPTER NINETEEN

Continuing to San Francisco and Vallejo, they were warmly greeted by Louise's Aunt Grace and Uncle George, who could not resist showing them their album of pictures of Jenny's earliest years. Duval's wineries in Napa were performing well, their newest vintages having won several medals in recent tasting competitions. The Mondavi Winery was thriving and still drawing admiring crowds to its twilight concerts in the vineyard.

After a brief visit to the gravesite of Louise's mother in San Francisco, they were happy to board their ship for the relaxing cruise across the Pacific. Nick was already familiar with life aboard a cruise ship, but to Louise, this opened up a whole new

world of organized pleasure. They swam
and sunbathed by day, dressed up and dined
in splendor in the evenings, and enjoyed a
variety of entertaining shows. Life at sea was
carefree and the six days to Hawaii passed all
too quickly.

Arrival at the Aloha Tower in Honolulu was
a spectacle in itself. Native boys surrounded
the ship and dived for coins tossed by the
passengers. A troupe of nubile hula dancers
swayed in greeting to the tunes of the Royal
Hawaiian Band, and dozens of local residents
presented their arriving guests with traditional
flower leis. Among them were Malia, Kimo,
and their two charming little girls. The scene
resembled a national holiday, dwarfing the
usual airport arrival.

Louise and Nick wanted to express their
gratitude for Malia and Kimo's role in
cementing their relationship.

"How could I ignore the strong
encouragement of attending your beautiful
Hawaiian wedding to make my move on
Louise?" joked Nick.

"Yeah, but brah, how come it took you guys

so long to tie the knot?" asked Kimo.

"Well," replied Nick, "that's a really long story, and we're only here for the day." And with that, he fished out his wallet and proudly showed the photo of their daughter Jenny.

"Oops," laughed Kimo, "I guess you folks really made hay in our Hawaiian sunshine."

"Yes," laughed Louise, "but it was more in the moonlight."

Malia told them that like most working couples, they really needed to get back to their jobs, but Nick insisted they all join him and Louise for lunch at the Willows restaurant.

"That's wonderful, how come you know about that place?" asked Kimo, in surprise.

"Nick always does careful research," answered Louise. "He told me it was the most lovely Hawaiian-style restaurant in town, and more like the Coco Palms than anything else in Waikiki."

Hailing a large cab, Nick took them all to lunch at the iconic Waikiki landmark, founded in 1944 and still preserved as a hidden tropical haven, in a garden setting around a palm-fringed lagoon, complete with colorful fish, and trickling waterfalls. The food was great, too, and the meal was topped off by a mountainous dessert of macadamia nut cream pie that had the two little girls cooing with delight. They explained that their names "Nani" and "Luana" translated in to "Pretty" and "Happy" respectively.

"How perfectly appropriate," remarked Louise.

Malia told them that she still worked part-time at the hair salon, while Kimo sang in a Waikiki club during the week and starred in his own show at the Coco Palms in Kauai on weekends.

"He's quite a big star these days," said Malia proudly. "Now before you go back to your ship, we have mementos for you."

The two children presented handmade necklaces they had strung together from puka shells they had personally collected from the Kauai beaches, and Malia gave them Kimo's latest recording of Hawaiian songs, featuring the famous "*Hawaiian Wedding Song*," and Kui Lee's romantic "*I'll Remember You*." Nick and Louise were moved to tears and embraced the whole family. "Mahalo nui loa. We shall always remember you, too," were their parting words, as they waved the happy little Hawaiian family a fond "Aloha" farewell, and returned to their ship.

With many other passengers, they ceremoniously threw their leis into the ocean, as they observed the Hawaiian custom that signified that one day they would return to the islands. Their parting had been quite an emotional one, and they continued to wave to the shore as the ship sailed out of the harbor on its way to their next destination.

Sailing south, they crossed the equator and the International Dateline, observed by the crew with a mischievous mock ceremony of dousing a fellow crew member and throwing him into the pool. All the passengers received a signed certificate marking the occasion.

CHAPTER TWENTY

As beautiful and exotic as were the
Hawaiian Islands, Louise was unprepared for
the pristine sight of the islands of Polynesia
as they were approached by their cruise ship.
The sight of Moorea in the early morning
mist was breathtaking as the ship sailed into
Cook Bay, named after the first European
explorer, Capt. James Cook—a Yorkshireman,
Nick of course had to note—who discovered
the tiny island. Their ship did not land there,
but continued to Bora Bora, for a
daytime excursion.

"The original name of the island," explained
Nick, "was Pora Pora, and in the Tahitian
language, that means 'first-born.' Rather
appropriate for us, don't you think, darling?

British missionaries arrived soon after and founded a Protestant church here," Nick continued with his history lesson, "and it was an independent kingdom until 1888 when the last queen was forced to abdicate by the French, who annexed the island as a colony."

"Hmm," said Louise, "rather sad, and rather like the way the Americans treated the last queen of Hawaii."

"During the war, Bora Bora was an important military supply base, and for a long time had the only international airport, but surprisingly its occupancy by American troops went uncontested and the base was closed at the end of the war. But enough history," said Nick, "They have a very unique hotel here, consisting of thatched roof bungalows built out over the water on stilts, and I want to take you there for lunch. It would be a great place for a vacation hideaway, but our ship is bound for Papeete, and we have such wonderful friends to meet there. Let's hope we can return here one day." Louise was already in seventh heaven and was happy to follow Nick wherever he led her.

For the other passengers, the cruise ended with a day in Papeete, the capital of Tahiti, but Nick and Louise were greeted with affectionate enthusiasm by Nick's lifesaving friends. They were crowned with head leis by the two charming daughters of Bruce and Tia, and joined later by Dr. Moreau— the people Louise most wanted to thank for rehabilitating Nick during his forced stay on the island. They checked into the Maeva Beach Resort for the next three nights and sat by the pool for an impeccably tasteful French lunch. "Don't eat too much," warned Bruce, "We have a royal feast prepared for you tonight, as so many of your old friends want to meet you Nick . . . and especially your lovely new bride."

The feast that night was indeed of royal proportions, in the form of a typical Tahitian luau, beginning with a torchlight ceremony and a troupe of Polynesian dancers. A bed of hot coals was laid out for the few intrepid men who demonstrated their ability to walk on them barefoot while dancing the Tamure to the chants of a high priest. Louise was awestruck at this brave spectacle.

The roast pig was taken from the imu and carved for the guests to the accompaniment of taro, sweet potatoes, lomi-lomi salmon, and a vast array of tropical fruits. For the squeamish there was barbecued chicken and beef kabobs and spicy dipping sauces of every variety. Liberal quantities of Mai Tais helped to enliven the proceedings, as many of the guests rose to dance with the enticement of the beckoning female dancers. Nick and Louise were forced to their feet to perform their own version of a Tahitian hula, with raucous applause and encouragement from the crowd. Louise looked gorgeous in a colorful pareo sarong, and Nick was draped by a laughing Bruce in a traditional skirt of similar colors. Bowing gracefully to the applause, Nick raised his hand for silence.

"My dear friends, I cannot thank you all enough for your wonderful hospitality to me and my beautiful wife. I owe my very life to you and you will always have a special place in our hearts."

There was more applause, and lots more

dancing and drinking continued into the wee hours, until Louise and Nick were finally allowed to return to their hotel for a night's rest. Next day they toured the island by "le truck," a convenient form of local transportation, which allowed them to visit the Gauguin Museum, formerly the house where the French Impressionist artist spent most of his years in Tahiti. Nick explained that the collection of paintings on display were merely excellent copies, as the originals had been sent to Paris for reasons of climate control and preservation.

The town center of Papeete, with its bustling waterfront location, boasted a colorful market place, numerous cafes, and gift stores, notably some offering the beautiful black pearls, which were the main economy of the islands.

"I used to dive for these and could have collected a sackful in Manihi," said Nick, "But I'd like you to visit the Musee des Perles where the exhibits will give you an interesting education as to how these precious gems are cultivated and farmed. Then we shall visit one

of the specialty jewelry stores where some
sophisticated French artisans have fashioned
them into sparkling necklaces and earrings.
Come with me and pick out your favorite set.
I want you to have them as a special wedding
present and souvenir of our visit."

"I already have a dozen souvenirs and
wonderful memories," replied Louise,
"but if you insist." She chose a stylish
combination of lustrous black pearls with
matching earrings.

"And for you, Nick, my present is a set of
pearl studs and cuff-links for your tuxedo."

"Now let's find something for the girls,"
she said. They moved on to another store
where they picked out two very colorful
Tahitian pareos, plus a pair of hand-painted
bedspreads appliquéd with flowers and
cultural symbols.

"I think the girls will appreciate these,"
she said.

"I'd like to take you to the hospital where
I spent so many months of care under Dr.
Moreau and his nursing staff," said Nick,
"and persuade him to join us for lunch. I

don't know how many of the original staff are still there—people don't move around very much out here—but I would like to pay my respects."

The good doctor was happy to spend time with the couple and drove them to a charming little restaurant on top of a hill which overlooked the entire harbor. They spent a lazy afternoon back at their hotel pool and later joined Bruce and Tia for a leisurely home-cooked dinner on the terrace of their home. Their stay in Papeete was coming to an end, but Nick sprang another surprise on Louise.

"I would love you to have seen Manihi," he said, "but there is no airstrip there and no hotel, so I am taking you to another small island, probably the most picturesque of all the Society Islands. It is called Huahine, and known as 'the garden island' because of its abundance of lush green tropical foliage, its diverse scenery of mountains, and miles of sandy beaches. We can rent a bicycle to get around and I can take you sailing and scuba diving." He added, "There is a remote tiny village called Maitai Lapita with a small thatched roof guest house where we can spend three more lazy days of solitude. We'll be lucky if we run into any other people there."

"Who needs people?" declared Louise. "I've had so much excitement these past three weeks, I'm ready for a complete rest before we return to civilization." And so they enjoyed the quietness of the tiny isle and took advantage of perfect weather for three sunny days and three moonlit nights, to reflect on their travel adventure and the future life awaiting them.

"I've never known such bliss, Nick darling," said Louise.

"Thank you for putting into words exactly the way I feel," replied Nick. In the course of their final blissful night under the stars, they submitted to their heartfelt feelings, and once again consummated their enduring love.

EPILOGUE

A little over five years had elapsed since Nick and Louise returned from their honeymoon. The agonizing memories of searching and discovering were behind them as they settled in to a more normal life of interesting, rewarding work and family pleasure in the laid-back town of Barbizon.

Pierre Duval and Nick Summers enjoyed an excellent working relationship as they deftly shared their business responsibilities with mutual respect. The introduction of new, smaller computers from IBM and Apple helped to eliminate a great deal of tedious paperwork and filing.

On a pleasant morning in June, the two families were gathered together to witness

the graduation ceremony at which Jenny
and Lilli were to receive their Baccalaureate
Certificates. Nick and Duval had combined
to present them with their own personal
computers as a reward for their achievements.

Sitting between Nick and Louise was a
bright-eyed and alert little boy of four-and-a-
half years they had named Henri, after Nick's
father and the closest they could think of to
remind them of their idyll in Huahine. The
line of students waiting for their certificates
was moving slowly towards the podium,
where each of them would curtsy and
proffer their cheeks for the double kiss in the
traditional French manner.

Nick's thoughts wandered back to his own
early life, the shock of losing his family,
partly tempered by the loving care of his
adoptive family in Yorkshire. He saw himself
graduating from the local grammar school,
followed by the more impressive graduation
ceremony at his university college. He
thought about his hard-working and lonely
years as a young adult in London, fortuitously
interrupted by his first chance meeting with

the captivating Louise. He reflected ruefully how strangers in Tahiti had saved his life and brought him back to reality, only to spend long and anguished years searching for Louise, culminating in their unexpected but joyous reunion.

His thoughts were suddenly interrupted by Louise tugging at his arm to draw his attention to their daughter, finally taking her place on the podium. He beamed with paternal pride and affection and, putting his arms around his wife and little Henri, he drew them closer to him. His life had now come full circle and he was thoroughly enjoying his role as head of his own family, vowing to devote himself to their welfare and happiness.

The ever-cheerful Pierre Duval was approaching them, the man responsible for their miraculous second chance. "Allons mes enfants," he cried, "A la fête! It is time for us to make the party."

It was indeed party time.

SECOND
CHANCE

ACKNOWLEDGMENTS

Writing a story and completing its manuscript is one thing. Converting it into book form and getting it published is quite a different adventure. Consequently, I am indebted to a select number of individuals for their advice and technical proficiency.

First, I am pleased to acknowledge the initial input of Kevin O'Donnell for his astute referrals, notably to Catherine Manabat for her proofing and editorial suggestions. Also to Ken Corr for his enthusiastic guidance and recommendations, and especially to Mike Bundlie for his design skills. All of them gave generously of their time and helped me achieve my objective.

ABOUT THE AUTHOR

Norman Sosner was born, raised, and educated in England. He lectured on History and Global Affairs as a young Education Officer in the Royal Air Force, while also taking an active part as Producer, Director, and Actor in Community Theatre.

Emigrating to the United States, the author met and married an English girl and together they pursued their love of international travel, organizing their own worldwide travel company, which over a period of 25 years took them to all five continents.

Taking early retirement, he devoted himself to assisting several arts and music entities with marketing programs which won him state and national awards for creative events and fundraising.

This novel is his first attempt at fiction, but Mr. Sosner is no stranger to the written word, having produced numerous brochures and newsletters on travel, music and the arts, as well as a broadcast series of wine chats and TV infomercials.

Finally settling with his wife and family in Hawaii, the author published his extensive memoirs and then turned his hand to this romantic novel. It chronicles the life of a young war orphan through the turbulent historic events of five decades, during which time he finds, loses, and eventually regains the love of his life.